A firm knock sounded on the back door.

Eden opened it to a tall, dark-haired man with deep-set brown eyes. A kernel of concern formed in her chest. "Can I help you?"

The man cleared his throat and shifted his weight. "Is this the Sinclair home?"

Eden debated whether to affirm his question. "Yes."

The man's brown eyes narrowed. "Is Owen Sinclair here?"

Eden's defenses heightened. No one came to visit anymore. Owen had few friends. "May I ask what your business is?"

The man's eyebrows rose as if offended. "Who are you?"

Eden stiffened at the authoritative tone of his voice. "Please state your business or I'll have to ask you to leave."

The man's jaw worked side to side. "I'm Blake. Blake Sinclair. Owen is my father."

Eden blanched. A chill shot up her spine, followed quickly by a jolt of anger. This couldn't be happening. The last thing they needed now was for her coldhearted brother-in-law to suddenly reappear. "What are you doing here?"

He shrugged. "I've come home."

Lorraine Beatty was raised in Columbus, Ohio, but now calls Mississippi home. She and her husband, Joe, have two sons and five grandchildren. Lorraine started writing in junior high and is a member of RWA and ACFW and is a charter member and past president of Magnolia State Romance Writers. In her spare time she likes to work in her garden, travel and spend time with her family.

Books by Lorraine Beatty

Love Inspired

The Orphans' Blessing
Her Secret Hope
The Family He Needs
The Loner's Secret Past
The Widow's Choice

Mississippi Hearts

Her Fresh Start Family
Their Family Legacy
Their Family Blessing

Visit the Author Profile page at LoveInspired.com for more titles.

The Widow's Choice

Lorraine Beatty

LOVE INSPIRED

INSPIRATIONAL ROMANCE

LOVE INSPIRED®
INSPIRATIONAL ROMANCE

Recycling programs
for this product may
not exist in your area.

ISBN-13: 978-1-335-58583-7

The Widow's Choice

Copyright © 2023 by Lorraine Beatty

For questions and comments about the quality of this book, please contact us
at CustomerService@Harlequin.com.

Love Inspired
22 Adelaide St. West, 41st Floor
Toronto, Ontario M5H 4E3, Canada
www.LoveInspired.com

Printed in U.S.A.

Only by pride cometh contention:
but with the well advised is wisdom.
—Proverbs 13:10

To the law enforcement community. We deeply appreciate your service and dedication.

Chapter One

Eden Sinclair positioned the cursor over the send button, then paused. Hopefully, this email would be the one that brought the heirs of the Beaumont estate together regarding the future of the historic home. Then again, it might just make matters worse.

Biting her bottom lip, she winced as she clicked and sent the email on its way. As the assistant director of the South Mississippi Preservation Society, she'd been put in charge of dealing with the current owners of the antebellum home. The six heirs had been bickering over the future of the house for nearly two years. Eden had tried everything she could think of to bring them together. Still, each had a vision for the home, and none were willing to compromise, which complicated the society's desire to purchase the home and restore it. Beaumont was historically significant to the small town of Blessing, Mississippi, and Eden was determined to save the unique structure.

Leaning back on the sofa, she exhaled a heavy sigh. If only there were more hours in the day or fewer obligations. Closing her laptop, she let her gaze drift to the view outside the large windows that ran the length of the cozy sitting area and kitchen in Oakley Hall. It, too, was a historic home and had been the Sinclair family residence since the late 1800s. She and her five-year-old daughter, Lucy, had moved in here after her husband, Mark, had passed away two years ago. A bitter swirl of anger and sympathy spurred her emotions. Would she ever come to terms with his duplicity?

Shaking off the sour mood, she allowed herself a moment to enjoy the winter camellias blooming in the backyard, their red-and-white flowers adding a welcome burst of color to the late January landscape. She would like to enjoy the quiet a little longer but knew there was no time to dillydally. Eden was due at work in half an hour. Rising, she moved to the kitchen just as friend and caregiver Jackie Gibbs entered with a plate in her hand and a scowl on her face.

"Old fool! I don't know why I put up with him. We should have him committed."

Eden smiled. She knew why they put up with Owen Sinclair. Because they loved him. Or rather, the man he *used* to be. The losses in her father-in-law's life had taken a toll and since the death of his oldest son, her husband, Mark, he'd lost all reason to live. A heart attack shortly after Mark's death had left Owen with a restricted lifestyle, which he'd fought tooth and nail. Depression had also set in, stealing much of his usual enthusiasm.

Thankfully, his latest project kept him occupied and reasonably stable. He'd purchased the historic Saint Joseph's Church and was creating a private museum dedicated to the history of Blessing, and he'd put her in charge of it. A mixed blessing.

"Then I guess we should be grateful for the museum. At least it keeps his mind occupied."

Jackie grunted. "Silly notion if you ask me."

Eden chuckled. She'd be lost without the woman. As an old friend of the family and a professional caregiver, Jackie had come to Oakley to nurse Owen after his illness. She'd quickly become like family, eventually moving in to help Eden as well. Eden had floundered since Mark died, trying to raise her daughter amid learning that her upright, responsible husband had left them financially destitute. It was only due to Owen's kindness that she and Lucy had a place to live with him in this old house.

Jackie dumped the toast into the trash and rinsed the plate. "I did manage to get one of his meds down him. He wants to see Lucy when she gets home from school. He adores that child. She's the sunshine in all our lives."

Eden couldn't agree more. Her daughter was always smiling, happy and eager to help. But also a constant source of worry, always looking around corners and climbing fences to see what lay beyond.

Jackie took a glass from the cupboard. "I've been meaning to ask, how are things at the museum?"

Eden eased into a chair at the breakfast table. "Not good. I can't be there full-time and things at work are so busy I can't get away like I did a few months ago. Owen has promised to find me some help, but he doesn't want to pay anyone, which leaves volunteers, and you know how that goes."

Jackie nodded in understanding. "The town is not too happy with Owen opening a private museum. He should have given that building to the historical society and let them manage things."

Eden didn't disagree. "I know, but it's the only thing he's interested in now and I don't want to let him down. But I don't know how much longer I can do it alone…"

Jackie poured a glass of water and held it up. "I'm going to see if I can get a few more pills down our bull-headed grouch. And I'll slip in a comment about the museum, too." She winked.

Eden smiled. "Good luck with that." She was beside herself with worry over Owen's health, mainly because he refused to take his medications. She and Jackie had tried all kinds of persuasions, but Owen had only dug in his heels. With his heart condition, he was supposed to avoid excitement of any kind. However, his volatile personality could explode at any moment, which made the danger of another heart attack an ongoing concern.

A shadow passed over the kitchen window and a firm knock sounded on the back door. Eden opened it to a tall, dark-haired man with deep-set brown eyes. He held a large duffel bag and gripped a cane in his right hand. A kernel of concern formed in her chest. "Can I help you?"

The man cleared his throat and shifted his weight. "Is this the Sinclair home?"

Eden debated whether to answer his question, but finally replied, "Yes."

The man's brown eyes narrowed. "Is Owen Sinclair here?"

Her defenses rose. No one came to visit anymore. Owen had few friends. "May I ask what your business is?" The man's eyebrows rose as if he was offended.

"Who are you?"

Eden stiffened at the authoritative tone of his voice. "Please state your business or I'll have to ask you to leave." The man's jaw worked side to side.

"I'm Blake Sinclair. Owen is my father."

Eden blanched. A chill shot up her spine followed quickly by a jolt of anger. This couldn't be happening. The last thing they needed now was for her cold-hearted brother-in-law to suddenly reappear. "What are you doing here?"

He shrugged. "I've come home."

The half grin he gave her lit the fuse on her irritation. "This hasn't been your home for twelve years. You're not welcome here."

He nodded slightly. "I expected that, but I'd like to see my father."

"He's not well. He can't have visitors." The man's demeanor shifted from pleasant to challenging and he squared his shoulders.

"And who are you and why are you in my father's house?"

Eden stood her ground. "I live here. I'm Eden Sinclair. Mark's…wife."

The man's attitude shifted again, his shoulders lowering and his gaze softening. "Mark. *Married.* I should have expected that. Where is he? I'll talk to him."

Eden fought the sting of tears that always formed when she thought of her husband. Whatever his faults, she'd loved him. "Mark died two years ago." The shock on the man's face gave her a twinge of satisfaction, which she promptly smothered. She needed to remember this was her brother-in-law. He was family.

"I…I didn't know. I'm sorry."

"Blake? Oh my word, is it you?" Jackie slid past

Eden and wrapped the man in a hug, speaking softly and rocking him back and forth. When the hug ended, she took his face in her palms. "It's so good to see you. So good."

Eden crossed her arms over her chest and waited. Jackie might be happy to see this prodigal son, but she had no use for the black sheep. She'd heard all about the younger brother's reckless, self-centered behavior and knew firsthand about the shattered lives he'd left behind when he turned his back on his family.

"Come in, kiddo. I want to hear what you've been doing. It's so good to have you home." She turned toward Eden. "Please pour a glass of sweet tea for our lost sheep."

Eden did as she was asked but every fiber of her being protested. Jackie and her brother-in-law sat down at the breakfast room table. After handing him the tea, she leaned against the counter. Blake glanced her way several times and she returned the look with a glare.

"It's good to be home and come across a familiar face. I haven't seen you since before Mom died. What are you doing here?"

"I live here now. I take care of the family." Jackie placed her hands over his. "Are you okay? You look pale and tired."

"It was a long trip here from California."

"Oh my, I should say so. And what about this?" She pointed to the wooden cane, and his leg, which was held stiff in front of him. "What happened?"

Eden didn't want to be curious, but she was. Blake was in his early thirties, five years younger than Mark. He should be in his prime. No doubt his years of wild living were to blame. She wiped that thought aside.

It wasn't in her nature to be harsh or judgmental, but when it came to her brother-in-law, the stories she'd heard did little to endear him to her. The way he'd cut his family out of his life made her blood boil. Family was the only thing that mattered in life.

Blake shrugged. "An old football injury."

Jackie grunted. "You didn't play football. You were the star pitcher of the baseball team." Jackie studied him a moment, then glanced at his leg. "What really happened to put you in such a state?"

He glanced at her again, then looked away quickly. His hands worked the handle of his cane, which was positioned between his legs. Eden waited for the big confession. Like maybe he'd jumped out of a plane or fallen off a mountain. She kept her arms crossed over her chest defensively. Whatever the reason, this should be good.

"I've been in rehab for the last year and a half."

Jackie reached over and laid her hand on his. "Rehab? You didn't get addicted, did you?"

He smiled and shook his head. "No. I took a bullet in my leg. Nearly lost it a couple times but the doctors pulled me through."

"A *bullet*! Oh, Blake, what were you involved in?"

He chuckled softly. "My job. I was a police detective. I was shot in the line of duty."

Jackie stared at him. "You were a policeman? All this time?"

"Pretty much. I was working for the Stockton, California, PD. But that's all over now. I got a medical discharge from the force. No more chasing bad guys for me. They tried to assign me a desk job but I turned it down. Not my style."

Jackie smiled. "A policeman. Your mama would be so proud."

He made a dismissive gesture. "She'd be the only one." He shifted his cane to his other hand. "I'd better go."

"Are you here to stay, BJ?"

Blake smiled. "I haven't heard that name since Mom passed. I don't know how long I'll be in town. That depends on Dad."

Jackie nodded. "I need to tell him you're here."

Eden couldn't remain silent. "No! I mean, what about his heart? This could be a terrible shock."

"What's wrong with his heart?" Narrowing his eyes, Blake looked to Jackie for an answer.

"He suffered a serious heart attack shortly after Mark died. We almost lost him." She paused and clasped her hands. "Since then, he's had to be careful and avoid any excitement. The whole thing has left him depressed and difficult to deal with."

Eden spoke up. "Having you suddenly pop up might be too much for him to handle."

Jackie sighed. "She has a point. I'll see if I can smooth things over before you see each other." She stood. "You wait here, and I'll go talk to him."

"I don't want to cause trouble. I just wanted to try and set things straight between us."

Jackie smiled. "I know."

As soon as the older woman left, Eden turned her gaze on Blake. "Don't you think it's a little late to try and fix things?"

"It's never too late to seek forgiveness."

The calm, smooth tone of his voice fueled her irritation. "You won't find any of that here."

Blake held her gaze, his dark eyes shadowed. "I know."

The man was insufferable. "Then why come back? Why now?"

"I had no place else to go and it was time."

Before she could respond, loud voices from the front of the house could be heard. As she'd expected, Owen wasn't pleased that his second son had returned. The voices grew louder, then suddenly stopped. Eden knew that meant Jackie had left the room. When Owen became unreasonable, she turned her back on him. It was the only thing that would get his attention.

When she returned to the kitchen, Eden knew they had reached an impasse.

"Your father is a bullheaded, hard-hearted old coot."

Blake nodded. "I didn't expect a warm hug and a fatted calf."

"Where are you staying?" Jackie asked.

"No place yet."

"I thought not. I'd offer you a room in the house but that might not be smart right now. You can stay in the studio for the time being. I'm sure I can get him to come around."

Eden stepped forward. "No, Jackie. He can't stay there, either." Eden glanced at Blake, who had stood and was leaning heavily on his cane. "I mean… It's too risky. If Owen should see him and not be prepared, his heart might not be able to take the shock."

"I realize that, but this is his *son*. His only living child. I'll not turn him out in the cold. They both deserve to face each other. And I'll not let Owen hide and pout for a week nursing his resentment, either. We're going to have supper together tonight. After that we'll let the Lord work it out."

"Jackie!"

She rolled her eyes at the sound of her name. "Oh dear. Round three is about to get underway. Eden, you help Blake to the studio. And I'll see if I can calm our grumpy old man down."

Eden started to protest but she knew Jackie was the only one who could deal with Owen when he was in this state. Lucy could lift his mood but she was at preschool this morning.

Eden walked past Blake and pushed open the back door. She was aware of him behind her, walking slowly and awkwardly across the long back porch with his stiff leg. She ignored the twinge of sympathy. Where was *his* sympathy when the family was grieving, and Mark struggled to keep the family business afloat?

"I know my way to the studio. My grandma lived there for years."

Eden ignored him. She strode down the long covered porch that jutted out from the east side of the historic home, stopping at the last door. The space had served as storage after she'd sold her home. The boxes were mainly filled with Mark's belongings that she hadn't known what to do with and hadn't been ready to give away. One day, she'd have to sort through it all, but not yet. It was easier to ignore it.

She unlocked the door and stepped back, allowing Blake to enter.

He glanced around, emitting a low whistle. "This doesn't look like I remember it. Grandma had a lot less stuff." He smiled over his shoulder at her. "She liked things clean, neat and free of clutter."

Eden pressed her lips together. He was already finding fault. She put the key on the table next to the door. "Most of these things belonged to Mark. You can put them in the old car barn if you want." She walked back along the porch, entered the kitchen, then stopped at the sink, emitting a loud groan of aggravation. "Unbelievable. Ungrateful. Arrogant."

"Are you talking about Owen or Blake?" Jackie came to her side. "What's the problem?"

Eden pushed away from the counter and gestured toward the back of the house. "Him. He's already complaining that the studio doesn't look like it did when his grandmother lived there."

Jackie shrugged. "That's understandable. Grandma Fuller was an artist. She was very persnickety about her home. Seeing the place filled with boxes would be a shock. He's come home to find everything changed."

Eden set her jaw and crossed her arms over her chest. "Why did he come home in the first place?"

"I think he felt it was time." Jackie gently stroked her arm. "What is it you're afraid of?"

"That he'll make things harder for Owen. He's not strong. He can't handle this kind of stress."

"Don't sell the old goat short. He's stronger than he lets on, and this might just yank him out of his depression. I'd rather have him feisty than lifeless."

"It's not just that. I've heard the stories about Blake's behavior—his reckless streak, the self-centered approach to everything. He's too disruptive."

Jackie held up a hand. "I know what you've heard and some of it *is* true, but don't you think we should give Blake the benefit of the doubt until we see otherwise? He's different. Calmer. Not the fidgety hothead he was as a young man."

"All I know is that Mark never had a good thing to say about him, and Owen would get enraged whenever his name was mentioned."

"I'm not denying there was bad blood between the three of them, but there are two sides to every story, and I think we need to hear Blake's side before we kick him to the curb."

Eden's anger eased and her conscience pricked. Tales of bad-boy Blake's escapades had been drilled into her from the moment she met Mark and had been underscored by her father-in-law. She didn't want to be unfair, but she wasn't about to risk Owen's health, either.

"I don't want Owen to be hurt. He and Lucy are the only family I have."

Jackie smiled and squeezed her hand. "And me."

Eden smiled. "Yes, of course."

Jackie patted her shoulder. "Just give the boy a chance."

"I'll try."

"Good girl. Now, I'm going back into the black bear's cave and see if I can convince him to see his long-lost son."

His son…the policeman. Eden couldn't ignore that fact. A wounded cop. Not the image she'd carried all these years. She had a tough time reconciling his job with his reputation. Was he telling the truth or was it a story meant to elicit sympathy so he could worm his way back into the family? What did he really want here?

Eden ran her palms over her face. The man had only

been here a few minutes and she was already suspicious of his every move. Jackie was right—she needed to give him the benefit of the doubt.

But how was she supposed to do that?

Detective Blake Sinclair watched Eden walk toward the house, stiff-backed and disapproving. Her resentment was obvious. He wasn't sure what his surprise sister-in-law had against him, but he expected he'd find out soon enough. She sure hadn't hesitated to express her opinions. However, he suspected her attitude was based on more than concern for his ailing father.

He turned to survey his new lodgings. The rooms had been added for his grandmother in her later years and consisted of a living room and kitchen at the front of the studio and two bedrooms with a bath in the back. The best feature was the front porch. When she wasn't painting or working on a craft project, Grandma would sit in her rocker and watch the seasons change.

He ran a hand down the back of his neck. So much had changed in his family since he'd left. Foolishly, he'd assumed everything would be the same. Instead, he'd learned his brother had died, his father was ill and he'd acquired a sister-in-law and a niece.

They may have gotten off on the wrong foot, but there was no denying that Eden was a very attractive woman. Her blond hair flattered her delicate features and highlighted the bluest eyes he'd ever seen. Mark always had an eye for the prettiest girl in the room. Though he'd usually been attracted to the cool, sophisticated types. Eden was more of the sweet, girl-next-door variety.

A sharp sting of grief jolted his mind. His brother

was gone. The loss augured deep inside. So many years lost, years that might have given them a chance to grow close again like when they were kids.

But he had a sister-in-law and a niece to get to know. Mark's family. Though he had a feeling forming a relationship with his brother's wife would be difficult. She'd been cautious when she'd greeted him, but after he told her his name, her expression had darkened with the suddenness of a summer storm. She had gone pale and swayed as if her knees were going to buckle. Mostly, she looked like she wanted to skin him alive.

He was definitely *not* welcome at Oakley Hall.

Blake scanned the studio again. The living room was serving as storage for random items and stacks of boxes. Eden had said they were Mark's things. He touched a box labeled Books. His brother had always been an avid reader, unlike him. Reading was a sedentary activity. He wanted action.

He trailed his hand across the box. What had taken his older brother's life so young? Perhaps Jackie would explain if his dad let him hang around long enough to find out.

Blake stopped at the bedroom window that looked out along the winding driveway. He'd had a bad feeling when he'd approached the house. The old home looked the same but tired and worn down. Like him. The house needed painting, the yard was overgrown and the roof was missing some shingles. He'd sensed then that something was very wrong. Owen Sinclair took as much pride in his home as he did his company. And Mark. His *perfect*, oldest son.

He shoved aside the old resentment. Maybe he should leave and not cause any trouble. No. He'd come too far and learned too much to back out now. He'd walked out of Blessing twelve years ago with no intention of ever returning. Yet here he was, the prodigal returned. He slipped his hands into his pockets and closed his eyes. Only there would be no rejoicing parent to run to greet him with open arms.

A dull ache began along his thigh, and he rubbed it vigorously to ease the spasm. He was feeling the effects of his two-mile walk from town to Oakley Hall. Blessing had grown in his absence, and the woodlands surrounding his home now boasted retail space and new homes. He suspected the big bicentennial this spring had caused the growth in the small town.

A zinger of pain lanced through his thigh. He groaned. He needed to sit. After carrying his grandma's old rocker from the living room to the porch, he eased into it. The gentle motion quickly drew away some of his fatigue and unearthed old memories of Grandma Fuller watching him and Mark playing ball in the yard. Blake had been a bit lost when she passed. She and his mom had understood his desire to break free from this town. Whereas Dad expected a stricter code of conduct and assimilation into the family business. Sinclair Properties was the only acceptable career for Owen's sons.

His stomach growled and the fatigue settled upon his shoulders again. He needed more than a rocker; he needed sleep. Back inside, he made his way to the bedroom and retrieved his meds from his duffel, downing two pills. His leg was throbbing. He'd overdone it today and his thigh was letting him know it. Wincing, he kicked off his boots, then sprawled across the bed and closed his eyes. An image of his surprise sister-in-law filled his mind. Why did she resent him so much? She'd behaved like a fierce protector of his father. She might be an obstacle to their reconciliation.

At least she was an attractive obstacle. He groaned and draped his arm over his eyes. It was not something he should be noticing about his brother's wife. No matter how lovely she was.

He rolled onto his side, buried his face in his pillow and drifted off.

A loud knock on his front door drew him from a restless sleep. It was still daylight. He couldn't have slept long. A quick glance at the clock showed it was late afternoon. He rose and started toward the living room only to have his leg start to buckle. He grabbed his cane.

Jackie stood on the front porch. "I came to deliver news. Not sure if it's good or bad."

He motioned her inside, but she shook her head. "I just wanted to let you know that your dad has agreed to have supper with the family this evening."

Blake frowned. "The whole family?"

"Yep. He's promised to mind his manners."

He huffed out a breath. "Right."

"Anyway, I thought you could use a heads-up." Her eyes narrowed. "You look tired. Everything okay?"

He nodded. "Fine. I overdid it today, that's all." Jackie looked skeptical but didn't challenge his comment.

Supper with the family. It should have made him happy. So why was his stomach tied in a huge knot? Probably because he doubted Owen could mind his manners for longer than a sip of sweet tea, but he knew he had to face his father eventually. The sooner that happened, the sooner he could move on with his life.

Blake stepped out onto the porch and eased into the rocker, his fingers worrying the carved handle of his cane. The big question was, where was his life headed now? Law enforcement was off the table. His bum leg ruled out many of the things he liked to do, but he could sort that out later. Right now, he had to figure out how he'd get through supper with his father.

A car pulled up and he watched as a little girl got out. Eden hurried across the patio and wrapped her in a hug, waving goodbye to the driver. This must be his niece. Lainey. No... *Lucy.* The thought took a moment to register. Mark, a husband and a dad. His heart ached for their loss. They must have been very happy. At least he hoped so.

From what he could see from the porch, the little girl was a carbon copy of her mother. They held hands as they walked to the house, Lucy's ponytail swaying playfully. The charming picture left him with an odd, hollow feeling in his chest. It also reminded him that the leg was still aching. He'd have to take it easy as much as possible today because tomorrow he had to get his life reinstated. A year and a half in a rehab facility had caused important parts of his life to lapse. His driver's license had expired, he had bank accounts to be activated and he needed to find a local physician to oversee his ongoing recovery. Now, however, he needed rest. If he was going to face his father shortly, he needed to be clearheaded.

Back in the bedroom, he stretched out, but sleep

didn't come. His mind was clogged with a hundred ways the evening meal could unfold. None of them good.

How would his father respond to his unexpected homecoming?

Chapter Two

Eden shut the kitchen door behind her, then looked toward the studio. Blake had been on the porch in the rocker watching when Shirley Kirby brought Lucy home. Eden had been aware of his presence but had chosen to ignore him. What did he expect to find here? And why had he come home after all this time?

She'd only heard about the bad-boy brother, had never even seen a picture of him, which was odd, come to think of it. But from the time she'd known Mark, she'd heard nothing good about Blake. So now that he was here it was only natural she'd be on her guard against this threat.

"Mommy, can Cuddles have a treat?" Lucy was stooped down petting her little Shih Tzu puppy. It had been a birthday present last month from Owen.

Eden turned from the window and smiled at her daughter. "I know what you really want is a treat for yourself."

Lucy grinned. "Ice cream."

"Well, you can have one of the little ones but nothing else until supper." She reached into the jar on the counter decorated with puppy paws and handed the small bone-shaped dog biscuit to Lucy. "That goes for Cuddles, too."

Lucy carried her ice cream to the table. "Who was that man on the porch?"

Eden's heart skipped a beat. She'd hoped the child hadn't noticed. She searched for an answer that would satisfy her little girl. She had no idea what Blake's position in the family would be, and she didn't want Lucy caught up in all the family drama. "He's visiting Miss Jackie."

"Oh."

Thankfully, Lucy was more interested in her treat than the stranger. It was times like this Eden wished Mark was here so they could discuss the best way to handle things. Though, he'd rarely been around most days. He'd been too busy at the office.

"There's my little Lucy Belle. Did you have fun at preschool?"

Lucy nodded. "Then I went to Addie's house to play."

"Wow, you had a big day." Jackie gave Lucy a kiss on the top of her head, then sat down. "That looks like good ice cream."

"It is. I ate it all. See…?" She held up the empty Dixie cup. "Mommy, can I go see Grandpa?"

"Sure. I think he's in his office." Lucy hurried off, Cuddles on her heels. Eden sank down into a chair and looked at Jackie. "What are we going to do about Blake?"

"I was going to ask you the same thing. What do you think of our long-lost son?"

"He's nothing like Mark."

Jackie chuckled and shook her head. "No, he is not.

If you didn't know they were brothers you'd never suspect. That was part of the problem. Blake was like his mother and that was hard for his dad and brother to understand."

Eden considered her friend's words. "They don't even look alike. Mark was so slender and elegant. Blake is more muscular, more the outdoors type."

"And more handsome."

Eden almost agreed but hot shame clogged her throat. "No one was as handsome as Mark."

Still, she couldn't deny that Blake possessed a kind of blatant masculinity that was hard to ignore. But somehow she would. *Not her type.* She pushed thoughts of Blake aside. She had bigger concerns. "I'm worried about what his sudden reappearance will do to Owen. His heart can't withstand this kind of emotional stress. Won't this be like adding fuel to a fire?"

"Maybe, but it's time that fire was put out." Jackie patted Eden's hand. "Don't worry, I won't put Owen at risk, but neither am I going to play along with this family feud or the pity party in which he's been indulging. I know what your father-in-law is going through. I've lost a spouse and I grieved, but eventually you have to accept it and start living again." She stood. "Which is why I'm starting a new campaign today. I'm calling it the B&O Railroad. Connecting the tracks between Blake and Owen."

Eden grinned. She loved Jackie's unquenchable spirit. "How do you plan on making that happen?"

"Hopefully tonight at supper. I'm fixing their favorite meal."

Eden didn't like Jackie's plan, but she also knew that the woman was the only one who could handle her father-in-law. All she could do was pray the meeting between father and son went peacefully.

Her anxiety was in high gear later as she filled the glasses with sweet tea and arranged one at each place setting. Everything was ready for the family meal. Secretly, she hoped that something would happen to change the plan. Anything would do. Owen changing his mind, a power outage, even a hurricane would be welcome, though in January that was impossible.

The timer on the oven beeped. Within minutes the food was on the table. With one last look to make sure everything was in its place, Eden walked to the family room. "Supper is ready." Not wanting to see Owen's re- action, she quickly turned and went back to the kitchen.

Lucy and Cuddles hurried behind her. "I'm hungry."

Eden smiled and helped her daughter onto her booster. "I like to hear that." She glanced at the door. Blake hadn't shown up. Maybe her prayers had been answered and he'd decided it was too difficult to meet his dad this way.

Before she could turn around, Blake tapped lightly on the door, then let himself in. Lucy greeted him.

"Hi. My name is Lucy. Who are you?"

Normally, Eden was proud of her daughter's friendly demeanor, but this was not one of those times.

Blake smiled. "I'm your uncle Blake."

She thought about that a moment. "What's an uncle?"

Blake leaned forward. "I'm your dad's brother."

She frowned as if the concept was too complicated, then glanced at her mother.

Eden set her jaw. "It just means we're family."

Blake held her gaze a moment before reaching out to pet Lucy's puppy. "Who's your friend?"

"He's Cuddles. He's a boy."

Blake nodded thoughtfully. "Good to know."

Behind her, Eden heard Jackie and Owen enter the kitchen together. She tensed. She did not want to be present when father and son saw each other for the first time in over a decade, but here she was literally standing between the two.

She watched as Blake looked at his father. His mouth was in a tight line, his dark eyes shadowed. Was that a hint of pain in the brown depths?

"Hello, Dad."

Owen grunted, yanked a chair out and sat down. Eden moved to take a seat, only to realize that she'd be next to Blake. Owen and Jackie were on the opposite side and Lucy was tucked between her and Owen. Wonderful. Not only did she have a front-row seat for this encounter, but she was also in the line of fire.

Owen kept his gaze lowered to his plate, his jaw working back and forth as if trying to control his emotions.

Jackie smiled. "I hope the chicken pie is good. It's been a while since I've made it. It's from your mother's recipe, Blake."

"Then it's bound to be delicious."

Owen started to reach for the bowl of green beans, but Lucy interrupted him. "Grandpa, we have to say the blessing, remember?"

Eden tensed. Owen's expression looked like it was the last thing he wanted to do, but he could never deny a request from his granddaughter. Lucy held out her hands. Owen took one and Eden took the other, only then realizing that she'd have to take Blake's hand as well. It took a full second for her to decide to accept the moment. Get the blessing over with and let go.

His hand wrapped around her fingers, warm and gentle, the contact creating a ripple in her pulse. Apprehension no doubt. Still, she couldn't ignore the surprising strength she found in his large hand. She'd expected his grasp to be weak.

Lucy said her favorite blessing. "God is great, God is good, let us thank Him for our food. Amen!"

Everyone chuckled at her enthusiastic amen. Before Eden could reclaim her hand, Blake released it like it was on fire. Apparently, he didn't want to be any more connected to her than she did to him. Fine with her. So why did she feel slightly offended?

Jackie started a conversation about Lucy's latest art project while passing around the food. Eden tried not to look between father and son, but as the minutes ticked by, she grew increasingly apprehensive. Surely this peace couldn't last for the entire meal.

Jackie finished her story, but no one took up the conversation. After a long silence, she tried again. "It's so nice to have the family together around the table."

Owen aimed his gaze at Blake. "It's the wrong son. It should be Mark. Not him."

Eden froze, shocked at Owen's harsh words, and felt a rush of sympathy for Blake. How awful to be reviled by your father. She looked at Blake, but his expression was unreadable. She braced herself. *Here it comes. The fireworks are about to begin.* If they got too heated, she'd have to take Lucy away.

Blake was silent a moment, then looked at Owen. "You're right. He should be here. But he's not."

The older man shook his head. "You're not welcome here. You're dead to me."

"I know that, too, but I'm not dead. I'm here and I want to try and make amends somehow."

"Impossible. You can't take his place."

Eden nearly choked on her bite of pie. She never expected to hear these things coming from her father-in-law.

Jackie patted Owen's arm and whispered softly, "Calm down. Take a deep breath."

"Jackie, this chicken pie is even better than I remembered."

Blake's comment drew a grunt from his father.

"It must be the only thing you remember. Did you forget where you lived? Who you were? Who you were supposed to be? Your obligations?"

Owen's tone grew angrier with each word.

Eden sensed Blake stiffen beside her and braced herself. His calm response surprised her. "Jackie, would you pass the corn?"

Owen set his glass down with a loud bang. "I'm talking to you."

"No, sir. You were interrogating me."

"Have you no answer?"

Blake set his fork down. "Yes. I never forgot where I lived. I found who I was and where I was supposed to be. And I met all my obligations."

"Not to your family."

"To *myself.*"

"Ha. You were always a self-centered brat." Owen fisted his hands on either side of his plate. "Why did you come back here?"

Blake didn't flinch at the cruel question. "It was time. I don't want to be at odds with you any longer."

"Too late for that. What did you hope to accomplish?"

"I thought we could be a family again," Blake answered. "And that I could help around here or lend a hand at the office."

Owen slammed a fist on the table, rattling the dishes. "Stay away from my business. You didn't want it when I needed you and I don't need you now. If you really want to help, then help her."

Eden blinked when her father-in-law pointed directly at her.

"She needs help at the museum if it's going to be ready for the bicentennial this spring. Make yourself useful."

Blake's shocked expression mirrored her own. "What? I mean… I'm not sure that I—"

"Just as I expected. You only want to help when it suits you. You want to mend fences, then prove it. Get yourself over to my museum and help Eden. You can start tomorrow."

"I can't be there tomorrow."

Owen waved off Eden's comment. "Then he can show up when you need him." Her father-in-law pushed back from the table and walked out.

Eden watched him leave, unable to speak for the tightness in her throat. Owen couldn't be serious. This was *disastrous*. She couldn't work with Blake. He'd be underfoot, complicating things and slowing her progress. Not to mention she didn't like the way he made her feel. Being near him left her confused and angry… and edgy. All the things she'd heard about him kept swirling in her mind. Only now she didn't know what to believe.

She looked at Blake, who had leaned forward with his elbows on the table, his hands clasped and resting against his forehead as if in prayer. Obviously, he wasn't eager to work with her, either.

Then he looked up, a sad smile flickering on his lips. "Sorry you had to see that. I should have been prepared, but I guess I expected too much."

"He shouldn't have said those things. I think he was just caught off guard by your sudden appearance after all this time."

Blake gave her a tolerant smile. "No. He's genuinely angry that I'm alive and his real son isn't. Nothing I can do about that." He raked his fingers over his scalp. "Well, looks like we're going to be working together."

She shook her head. "No, really, it's not necessary. I'm fine." Eden searched for a way to avoid this plan. "Owen didn't mean what he said."

Blake made a skeptical grunt. "I've known him longer than you and I recognize an order when I hear one."

She knew it, too, but was unwilling to agree so quickly. "The museum is on track. I'm behind at work so I can't spend as much time there as I'd like. I only have weekends to devote to it, and the evenings I like to spend with Lucy."

He frowned. "The museum isn't your regular job?"

"No. I work for the local Preservation Society. The museum is a part-time job." He studied her a moment as if wanting reassurance. "The museum will be done in plenty of time."

Blake pushed up from the chair using the tabletop for support. "I know it will. You and I will make sure of it." He grasped his cane. "Just let me know when to report to work. I'll be there." Then he turned and walked out.

Eden stared at the door, wishing she'd turned the man away this morning. Owen's command had turned her life upside down and she had no idea how she'd set things right again.

Lord, why did You send this man into my life? I can't handle this now. Please send him away.

She released the tense breath she'd been holding and shifted awkwardly in her seat, wondering how to proceed. The blowup was over. It hadn't been as physical as she'd expected but crueler than she'd imagined.

She ran through the scene again in her mind, puzzled by what hadn't happened. For years she'd heard about the epic battles between Blake and his father. Stories of the door slamming, fists pounding, nose-to-nose arguments. Even coming to blows at one time, but that hadn't happened. Instead, Blake had responded by calmly deflecting Owen's ugly words. Why hadn't he exploded?

On the other hand, her father-in-law had been angrier and viler than she'd ever seen him. The hateful things he'd said sparked a surprise sympathy in her for Blake. In all the years Eden had known Owen, she'd never heard him like this. Since his heart attack, he'd become easily irritated or frustrated when things didn't go well, but never so hateful and cruel.

Sighing, she watched through the large windows as Blake made his way along the porch to the studio. He looked defeated. His shoulders were slumped and he leaned heavily on his cane as he walked. Despite herself, she felt for him. Was Jackie right? Was he a different man from the one described to her over the years? She'd always chalked Mark's resentment up to sibling rivalry. But now she wondered if there was more to it.

Mark had always said his brother was a charmer, able to sway people to his side with a smile and skillful manipulation. Apparently, that was true because here she was after barely twelve hours in his presence, and she was feeling sorry for him. That said, she reminded herself he'd been a detective, wounded in the line of duty, which meant there must be more to him than the coldhearted man she'd heard about.

She stood and started to clear the dishes away. Setting the plates on the counter, she stared at her palm. She could still feel the touch of his hand and the way his fingers had curled around hers at the dinner table, not tight, just firm. Secure. It had been a very odd reaction.

She shook off the memory. Maybe this confrontation would convince Blake he wasn't wanted, and he'd move on. He'd made his attempt at reconciliation, and it had failed. End of story.

Blake stood in the doorway of the studio, his shoulder pressing against the frame. His first meeting with his father had been worse than he'd expected. Though why he should have anticipated anything else was ridiculous. He'd pinned his hopes on the passage of time softening the old man's heart.

He stared at the kitchen window, where he could see Eden clearing off the table. His one bite of chicken pie had been delicious. He hadn't been able to eat after his father's outburst. His chest had tightened like a vise as old memories choked off his air. The yelling, the ugly words that would escalate until his mother would physically come between them and defuse the situation. Most of the time it worked, but toward the end, she was too weak to keep the peace. He blamed that on Owen. His father always put his own concerns ahead of everyone else's.

Coming here might have been a mistake, but his desire to set things right with Owen was still his driving force. He wasn't ready to give up so soon. Not until it was completely hopeless. He'd known hopelessness in his life, and he wasn't there yet.

He had to keep trying, but he needed to keep the fights away from Eden and Lucy. He glanced at his hand. The memory of holding her hand during the blessing lingered. He could still feel the silky softness of her skin. Strange. He'd never known that sensation before. Not even with his ex-fiancée, Monica. Eden's touch was like a brand on his palm. It had given him a moment of connection, of being part of the family again.

He looked at the kitchen once more and saw that Jackie had joined Eden as they worked together. He hoped they saved some of that pie. He might be able to have it for lunch. Or he'd try to sneak back into the house later after everyone had gone to bed. His stomach rumbled. He was really hungry. Blake hated that the meal had been ruined for the others, but then Owen was good at creating drama.

He went inside, noticing the boxes he'd shoved to one side. Tomorrow he'd carry some to the old car barn. He needed more room if he was going to stay here. Despite the disagreement this evening, he wasn't ready to leave Blessing. He wasn't ready to say goodbye to the rest of the family, either. He'd been alone a long time. It had been four years since Monica had called off their engagement. He hadn't seen it coming. He should have, but the shock had wounded him deeply and had pushed him toward taking more risks in his job, which had led him to his current situation.

Being back home, even with his dad's rejection, was what he needed right now. He needed the comfort of familiar surroundings. Ideally, he'd like to have been in his old room, but the studio was almost as good. He'd spent a lot of time here visiting his grandma. Jackie was like a second mother to him. She'd been his mother's close friend and her son Tony had been Blake's best buddy all through school. And finding Eden and Lucy was a happy surprise.

As he walked past the box marked Books, he noticed it also said Personal. Intrigued, he pried it open and pulled out a file folder stuffed with paper. Below it was a small stack of books, mainly software tutorials. Underneath them was a laptop. He pulled it out just as a knock came on his door. He laid it back in the box and went to answer. "Eden."

She looked uncomfortable, her hands fidgeting nervously. "I just wanted to say that I'm sorry for the way Owen behaved at supper. It was… I've never seen him like that before. The things he said to you were cruel."

He smiled, caught off guard by her words. Earlier her blue eyes had shot daggers at him, yet now she was expressing sympathy. She must be a woman of deep compassion. "That's kind of you to say, but he wasn't as angry as I'd expected."

She bit her lip. "He's always been so sweet and kind

to me and Lucy, and he and Mark always got along so well. I don't understand this side of him."

Blake nodded. No need to ruin her opinion of Owen. "That's because Dad and Mark were cast from the same mold. My father and I never could find common ground."

She studied him a moment, as if trying to understand. "And you and Mark?"

How much should he share? There was no reason to tarnish his brother's memory. "We got along great until he was about twelve. That's when he decided to follow in Dad's footsteps, and we drifted apart. We saw the world differently. That's all." She nodded but something in her eyes made him take a closer look. Worry? "Don't worry about Dad and me. I'm going to give reconciliation a good try, but if I can't make that happen, then I'll move on. I won't disrupt the family forever. I don't want to burden you or Lucy with this mess."

She nodded. "Thank you for not making the situation worse tonight. I was prepared for—" She stopped, her cheeks turning pink, and she looked down.

Blake smiled. "You've heard about the old donnybrooks, huh? Well, I've learned a few things over the years. Patience being one of them."

She held his gaze a long moment as if she was trying to look inside him. He told himself to turn away, but he got caught up in the warmth of those blue eyes and it was hard to break eye contact.

"Well, it's getting late…" she murmured.

"Wait." He spoke without thinking. "Before you go, I suppose we should talk about my helping you at the museum."

"Not now. Maybe tomorrow."

"All right," he replied, trying to mask his disappointment.

"Good night, Blake."

He watched her walk back to the house, unable to take his eyes off her. She was an interesting woman. He grunted and shut the door. Her concern for his feelings had left a warm sensation inside his chest. Mark had married an amazing woman. Beautiful, smart and caring. Not the type he would have expected him to choose. But then, his brother had undoubtedly changed over the years the way he had, and the way Owen hadn't.

Eden had given him a small kernel of hope that he could be reconciled with at least one member of his family. He'd like to be friends with his sister-in-law. Especially since they'd be working together at the museum. The last thing he wanted was to stir up more division in the family.

Perhaps her unexpected display of understanding was a good sign that she didn't want him drawn and quartered after all.

Chapter Three

Blake eased open the back door of the main house the next morning, scanning the room. No one here. He'd found a coffee maker in the studio kitchen but no coffee so he decided to risk running into the family in search of a cup and maybe a biscuit or roll.

The smell of fresh brew drew him to the end of the kitchen counter. Everything he needed, cups, spoons, sugar and cream, was right there. The first sip was pure nectar. He closed his eyes and savored the taste, letting the warmth chase away the chill in his bones. Yesterday the weather had been balmy and sunny. A front had moved through overnight, bringing colder temperatures for the day, but tomorrow would be warm again. He'd forgotten how erratic winter in the South could be.

"Hi, Uncle Blake."

He glanced down and smiled at his niece. She looked adorable with her ponytail all askew and a big smile on her face. He might enjoy this uncle thing. "Good morning, Lucy."

"Are you going to fix me breakfast? Miss Jackie always makes me pancakes."

"Really? Well. I suppose I could do her job this morning. If you help me."

Lucy nodded, smiling. "I like to help."

"Perfect. Can you show me where everything is?" After a few misdirections, Blake located a skillet and the ingredients for basic pancakes.

Lucy dragged a stool over to the counter and climbed up. "I'm a good stirrer."

He chuckled and handed her the spoon. "Then you should do the honors."

Within a few minutes, the pancakes were being piled on a plate and carried to the table.

He'd made them silver dollar–size to amuse Lucy. They were halfway through the first batch when Eden showed up. The look of shock and surprise on her face would have been entertaining if he hadn't been so aware of her attitude toward him. He stopped midbite and waited for the scolding to begin. He didn't have long to wait. "What are you doing?"

He smiled, hoping to dilute her irritation. "I was hungry, so I made pancakes. Lucy was hungry, too."

"Uncle Blake makes baby pancakes. See. Aren't they cute?"

Eden's jaw slid side to side. "So, you just made yourself at home?"

Blake met her gaze. So much for the friendly approach. "It's still my home."

"Mommy, I helped, too. I stirred."

Eden placed a possessive hand on Lucy's head. "That was nice of you to help, sweet pea."

She may have been speaking to her daughter, but her eyes were on him. "You can't make amends by fixing breakfast."

"I wasn't trying to. I was hungry. That's all."

"You want some baby pancakes, Mommy? They're yummy."

"No, thank you."

"Can Cuddles have one?"

"No. It's not good for him."

Jackie strode in, a big smile on her face. "Good morning. It's good to see you sitting here, BJ. Oh, and you made pancakes." She looked at Eden. "Blake and his mom would have them every weekend. They were the only ones in the family who liked them."

"Mark hated pancakes."

Blake saw Eden's cheeks redden, as if she hadn't meant to say that out loud.

Jackie nodded. "He and Owen preferred French toast."

Jackie kissed Lucy on the top of her head and touched Eden's shoulder as she came toward Blake and bent and kissed his cheek. "I'm glad you're making yourself at home, BJ." She moved to the coffee maker and poured a cup. "Did you sleep all right? The studio hasn't been lived in for a long time."

He glanced at Eden, but she'd turned her back and was staring at the orange in her hand. He forced his gaze to Jackie. "I rearranged a few things. It was fine and the bed was comfortable. I slept like the proverbial log."

"Good. I'll bring you fresh linens today and if you'll make a list, I'll pick up a few groceries." Jackie pursed her lips. "You certainly need to eat better. You look like a scarecrow. We need to fatten you up."

Blake smiled. "I remember what a good cook you were. I used to find any excuse to eat at your house."

"You and all of Tony's friends, as I recall."

He took another bite of pancake. "How did you end up living here, Miss Jackie?"

"I'm a caregiver now and when Owen became ill, I came in to help. Eden was working full-time and caring for Lucy. We all sort of clicked and I ended up moving in. It's been a blessing for all of us." She patted his shoulder. "Maybe it will be for you, too."

Blake doubted that. Between his father's unforgiving attitude and Eden's resentment, he feared his time at Oakley would be short. He changed the subject. "Is Paul Grayson still the manager at the Blessing bank?"

"He is."

"Good. I need to get some things taken care of." He rose and carried his plate to the sink. Eden drew away as he came near. Her bitterness toward him ran deep, and he wanted to understand why. He walked to the door, then turned back. "Eden, let me know when to report for work." She shot him an angry glare. He grinned and opened the door.

Lucy waved at him. "Bye, Uncle Blake."

"Bye, Lucy. Bye, Cuddles." He glanced at Eden, but her expression was much the same as it had been. *Disapproving.* It was going to take more than pancakes and a smile to forge their relationship.

Eden wiped the sticky syrup from Lucy's hands and carried her empty plate to the sink.

"Is Uncle Blake going to be here every morning? I like his pancakes."

She wanted to reply with a firm no, but she had no idea how long he'd hang around. A wave of unwelcome sympathy surfaced once again. He'd suffered a serious gunshot wound. Maybe coming home was something he needed.

Jackie refilled her cup. "I should have guessed BJ would end up in law enforcement."

Eden hated that she was curious. "Why is that?"

"Blake was a lot like his mom. Angela loved helping others. She was always volunteering for one thing or another. That's how we became so close. We both volunteered at the food bank and at Madeline's Clothes Store. She had a huge heart."

"I thought Blake was a wild child."

"He was rambunctious, always looking to try something new, wanting to see what was over the next hill. But he was never in trouble."

That information didn't mesh with what she'd always heard. "I don't understand."

Jackie plucked a muffin from the stand in the middle of the table. "Owen expected his sons to follow in his footsteps. The plan was that they would get a business degree and join the company. But Blake never wanted that. He was taking criminal justice classes and Angela made sure Owen didn't know. When she died, it all came out and the relationship between BJ and Owen fell apart. Owen felt Blake had betrayed the family. He delivered an ultimatum. Come to work for the company or get out. Blake left and that was that."

Eden shook her head, trying to understand. "Mark always said Blake was the one who had walked out without even a goodbye. He said it broke Owen's heart."

"I'm sure it did, but not in the way you think. He was heartbroken because his big dream of having both his sons in the company was shattered." She stood and went to the sink. "You know how much I care for your father-in-law, but he's always had a selfish streak. Angela was the only one who could temper it, especially when it came to BJ. But after she was gone, there was nothing to keep the pair from locking horns."

Eden couldn't deny that Owen had a one-track mind about certain things. He and Mark had both been workaholics when it came to Sinclair Properties, but she hadn't thought of it as selfish. However, maybe she hadn't been seeing him clearly. Her perceptions about Blake were taking a hit. "Why do you call him BJ?"

"It's what Angela always called him. Blake Jonathan. BJ."

"Oh." She brushed hair from her forehead and shoved aside her curiosity about her brother-in-law. "All I know is that whenever Blake's name came up, neither Mark nor Owen had anything good to say. They only talked about his contempt for family and his irresponsible lifestyle."

Jackie grimaced. "Deep down I think Owen felt guilty for the way he ordered Blake away, but he's a proud man and it is difficult for him to admit when he's been wrong."

Eden chafed at the observation. "You make him sound so self-centered."

"Right now he is." Jackie touched her hand. "He's stuck in his grief. Losing Mark was the end of his big dreams."

Eden teared up. She understood. The loss had been unbearable at times. If she could have shut down and hid in the house the way Owen had done, she would have, but she had a job and a child to take care of. "Can you blame him?"

"Yes, I can blame him, and no, he hasn't lost a dream.

Blake is here. He's a Sinclair, too. And you and Lucy are Owen's legacy, but all he can see is that one big dream is gone. Sometimes I want to shake his head off his shoulders. The stubborn old man needs to see into the future. I'm hoping Blake will force him to do that."

Eden was hoping Blake would see how unwelcome he was and leave. She bit her lip, immediately regretting the unkind thought.

Jackie stood. "It's my day to get Lucy to preschool. I've got errands to run so I'll see you later."

A glance at the clock told Eden she had nearly an hour before she had to be at work at the Preservation Society. That gave her plenty of time to work on cataloging some of the museum pieces Owen wanted on display.

Opening her laptop, she got to work, grateful that she had plenty to keep her mind off her brother-in-law. Movement out the window drew her attention. Blake was sitting on the porch steps outside the studio, his hands clasped on top of his cane, gazing thoughtfully out across the lawn. It was hard to find any family resemblance between the brothers.

Mark had been supremely confident, self-assured and controlled. Everything he did was neat, precise and planned. He'd been handsome, with sharp features and hawklike eyes. Even his wardrobe was crisp and sophisticated. Mark always made her think of the men in suit advertisements. Lean, neat and classically handsome.

Blake, on the other hand, was a different kind of attractive. With his strong features and deep-set, probing dark eyes, he was the very picture of the rugged, outdoors male. His hair was dark brown, and he had a lazy smile that captured your attention and highlighted his chiseled jawline. It was easy to see how he earned his reputation as a charmer.

The differences between the two brothers extended far beyond their looks. Mark had been a driven man, always focused on the next thing. He had a way of commanding the world to bend to his will. Much like Owen. However, Blake had a more easygoing way about him, as if he took life as it came. No doubt it was a quality that came in handy in his career in law enforcement.

Eden jerked her attention back to the computer screen. Why was she making comparisons? There was nothing about her brother-in-law that was admirable. Certainly not his ability to cut his family out of his life, then pop up suddenly and think he could fix years of neglect and estrangement with a pancake breakfast.

Yet, her mental image of Blake was finding it hard to align the man with the things she'd always heard about him. She pressed her hands against her warm cheeks, trying to chase away the guilt over her thoughts. She'd truly believed what Mark had told her about his brother. While he may not be the villain she'd expected, she couldn't forget what he'd done. Any man who would turn his back on his family to chase a reckless existence didn't deserve her sympathy. Then her conscience mocked her. Blake *hadn't* been living a frivolous life. He'd been a policeman. He'd served the public and taken a bullet in the process.

Was she judging him too harshly?

"Time will tell, girl." The man was still a stranger to her, and she wasn't going to change her opinion on twenty-four hours of exposure. Sooner or later, he'd show his true colors.

Curious, she stood and moved closer to the window for a better view. As she watched, Blake rose and started walking toward the old barn. Why would he be going there? It was filled with junk, as far as she knew. What was he up to? Impulse took hold and she headed out the back door to question him. He'd disappeared inside before she caught up with him. Filled with suspicion, she stepped inside. "What are you doing?"

He turned and smiled. "Hello, Eden. I'm looking for something."

"Obviously. What? And who said you could snoop around the property?"

His smile widened. "I did."

She'd expected him to stop and explain, but he kept moving farther into the gloomy space. The man had no shame. "What are you looking for?"

"A treasure."

Eden mentally rolled her eyes. "There are no hidden treasures here."

He grinned and waved a finger. "Ah, you might be surprised. Though, it's only a treasure to me."

Blake moved behind an old wagon and a stack of plywood kept on hand for hurricane season. "Bingo."

She wound through the odds and ends and found him in the far back corner. She watched as he pulled a large tarp away, revealing a dusty old motorcycle. "What's that?"

He grinned widely as if he had truly found a treasure. "That is Roxy. Roxy, meet Eden."

She frowned and shoved her hands into her sweater

pockets. "I'd hardly call an old rusty motorcycle a treasure."

"She may not look like much now, but she's a rare beauty. All she needs is a little spit and polish, new tires and she'll be good to go."

"I might have known you'd have a bike."

"Why is that?"

There was a challenging look in his eyes. She raised her chin. "Mark always said you were a daredevil."

"He did, huh? Well, he's wrong in this case. Roxy belonged to my Grandpa Fuller. My mother's dad. He got this bike from a friend and he and I spent the summer I was fourteen fixing it up. He left it to me when he passed." He brushed his hand slowly over the seat. "Best time of my life. Special memories."

Eden's protective feelings for Owen swelled. "No memories from your father?"

He shook his head. "Sinclair men were only interested in work. Not family or hobbies."

Eden bristled, insulted at his implication. "They had a strong work ethic. They were building something important."

"True, but what good is it if it blinds you to the needs of your family?"

Eden didn't want to pursue that topic. "So, what are you going to do with it now that you've found it?"

Blake set his hands on his hips. "Clean her up and make her hum again."

"And ride off into the sunset." She hadn't meant to sound so hopeful. Her cheeks warmed.

He held her gaze a moment, then tapped his bad leg. "Don't think that would be a good idea. You need two good legs to make her run."

Eden swallowed the lump in her throat. She should have thought of that.

Blake replaced the tarp over the bike and came toward her. "I wouldn't believe everything Mark told you. He and Dad have a certain way of looking at things. Especially the past."

She raised her chin and looked him in the eyes. "He was my husband. I think I'll take his word over yours."

He came toward her. "One thing I learned as a detective was that five people can observe the same incident and yet each give a different account. The truth lies somewhere in the mix. You have to take the time to dig it out." Blake cleared his throat. "Well, I'm off to town. Have a good day."

He walked past, leaving her in the dim barn with thoughts swirling like dust mites in her mind. He was a very confusing man.

She stepped outside to see him pick up a small backpack and his cane and start walking down the driveway. She glanced around. She'd assumed he had driven here, but she realized she didn't remember hearing a car yesterday. Had he walked here from town? Is that what he planned to do now?

She hurried after him. "Blake!" He stopped and looked back. She gestured for him to wait, then went inside the house, grabbed a set of keys, then hurried toward him. He looked puzzled. She couldn't blame him. Eden hadn't intended to be kind, but after learning of his injury, she couldn't allow him to walk the two miles to town on that leg. She handed him the keys. "Mark's pickup is parked in the new garage. I'm sure he'd want you to use it. It's just sitting there. I haven't taken the time to sell it."

Blake studied her a moment, then smiled, causing a blip in her pulse. She pressed her lips together.

"Thank you. I appreciate this. I'm not sure my brother would be in agreement with this loan, but I'm not one to pass up a blessing."

He tossed the keys into the air, grabbed them, then turned and walked to the garage. Eden turned and made her way quickly to the house, not wanting to see Blake behind the wheel of her husband's beloved vehicle. She was already regretting loaning him the truck. Because, no matter what he'd been through, she was *not* going to get chummy with the man. It would break Mark's heart. The thought quickly followed that he hadn't thought about her heart when he'd left her penniless and devastated at his betrayal.

Still, her first loyalty was to her husband. Blake would be gone soon enough, then she could get back to her job of saving the Beaumont house. She tried not to think about the time wasted on Owen's private museum that could have been spent on negotiating the purchase of the historic home. That's where her heart was. Saving old homes had always been her goal. But she loved Owen dearly; he was family, and she was determined to see his dream through no matter what.

Even if it meant working with Blake.

Eden's unexpected consideration swirled in Blake's thoughts during the drive into town. It had been nice seeing kindness in her eyes instead of the resentment that was usually there. He suspected much of her low opinion of him was due to his brother. What had Mark told her about his younger sibling? He knew they hadn't been close for a long time, but he'd never suspected his brother held such strong feelings against him. It must have started after he left the family and no doubt his dad had added to the rift over the years.

There had to be more to Eden's animosity, he just needed to find out what. He didn't like seeing the look of anger in her eyes. He wanted to see her smile like she did whenever she looked at Lucy. His adorable niece was a miniature version of her mother. Seeing them together always made him smile. Lord knows he'd had little to smile about in the last few years.

Maybe he could find a way to win her over by helping at the museum. Though he wasn't sure how he felt about working with her so closely, he couldn't deny he found her to be an intriguing woman. Strong, kind-hearted and loyal to a fault. Not to mention beautiful.

His brother had picked a special lady. A sting of realization hit him. Eden was his brother's wife. His widow. He needed to keep his thoughts about her purely platonic. Turning on his blinker, he pulled into the bank parking lot. Nothing like cold financial matters to keep a man's thoughts in line.

Hours later, Blake turned the truck toward Oakley Hall. He'd accomplished a lot today. His finances were in order, his driver's license renewed, and he'd met with a physician about his leg. His last stop had been at the church to renew his friendship with Pastor Miller. He'd need a spiritual specialist as much as he needed a medical one.

He turned on the radio and tapped his fingers on the steering wheel in time with the music. He almost had a real life again. As he drove past the old Saint Joseph's Church, he saw the new sign declaring it the Blessing History Museum. He wasn't looking forward to working there. He'd never enjoyed history. Especially with a woman who despised him. But when Owen Sinclair gave a command, it wasn't disobeyed.

Back home, Blake stopped the truck near the new garage and leaned forward to peer out the windshield. Eden and Lucy were holding hands and walking Cuddles across the lawn. He smiled. The chill of early morning had evolved into one of those sweet Mississippi winter days that felt more like early spring. He would like to join them and stroll between the trees. Had Mark realized how blessed he'd been? A beautiful, loving wife and sweet little girl to call his own.

His chest tightened. Those were things he would probably never experience for himself. He'd have to be content to witness them from a distance. He grunted softly as he got out of the truck. Coveting someone else's life wasn't something he'd ever indulged in. His life had been too full to long for more. But he was starting to envy his brother and the life he'd had with Eden and Lucy. A hot rush of blood scorched his veins. He had to stop these feelings from getting out of hand.

Slamming the door closed with more force than necessary, Blake retreated to the studio, glad that Eden and Lucy had already gone inside. He'd found himself wanting to watch them together. Not a good habit to develop. He had to watch his p's and q's while he was here. Because he didn't want to create any new awkward situations. Especially with Eden.

He winced. His leg was complaining. He'd walked a lot today and it was time to rest.

Blake headed toward the bedroom, noticing that there were bags from a local grocer on the kitchen counter. Jackie had come through. He could eat in his room and avoid the main house, he thought with relief as he stretched out on the bed. Though isolating himself wouldn't accomplish what he'd come here to do, which was to settle things with his dad.

Blake draped his arm over his eyes in an attempt to sort out the tangled mess he'd uncovered at Oakley Hall. He wasn't sure how to approach the various conflicts. All he knew was that he couldn't sort it out on his own. He needed someone with greater wisdom than he possessed. He might need a visit to the Blessing Bridge to untangle his confusing thoughts. The complications he'd found here were overwhelming.

Unable to still his troubled thoughts, Blake rose and went into the living room and fixed a glass of tea, then glanced at the stack of boxes near the door. Mark's things. Driven by a need to understand, he placed one box on the coffee table and opened it. He had so many questions. Why was Eden living with Owen? What had caused his brother's death? There was always an impression of secrecy when Mark was mentioned.

He sorted through one of the file folders, but it only held the usual company papers. After lifting out the laptop, he opened it and booted it up. While he waited, he examined a small datebook. Why his computer-savvy brother would have such an old-fashioned item intrigued him. He leafed through the pages, skimming the odd notations. Dates, numbers and appointments were all scribbled on the pages, but none of them made any sense.

When the laptop was up and running, he scanned the various files. Some were familiar names of properties Sinclair managed. Others were names he didn't know, but then his dad was always taking on new cli-

ents who wanted him to manage their buildings or con-
dos. It was one of the reasons Blake had left. Keeping
track of payments and tenants was the most boring
thing he could think of. Numbers in neat rows and
balance sheets with every penny accounted for were
more to Mark's liking.

Give him a good criminal collar any day.

Digging through the boxes only created more questions. There was still plenty of daylight. Maybe this
was a good time to see to his spiritual dilemmas, and
the best place to start was a visit to the Blessing Bridge.

A short while later he pulled to a stop in the parking lot. A large sign marked the location now officially
called the Blessing Bridge Prayer Garden. The bridge
had become a destination for the residents in the mid-
fifties after a mother prayed for healing from polio for
her son. When he recovered, people started coming to
the site to lift up their prayers.

Blake started down the path, which was covered
in fine gravel and neatly trimmed. The area had been
landscaped with perfectly placed flowers and benches,
creating a picturesque park. Years ago, when he used
to come, the grounds had been natural and untouched.
He'd practically forged the path himself with his fre-
quent visits. It was the only place he could come to
fully escape the dark shadows of home.

He stopped at the top of the arched bridge and leaned
on the rail, taking in the changes. The park was lovely
and peaceful, but he preferred the primitive state it
used to be in. It suited his mood back then. His mind
was wild and unruly. Pieces of his spirit were broken
like the limbs and branches that cluttered the ground.
He always left feeling hopeful, but also more deter-

mined to escape Blessing and the Sinclair name as soon as possible.

Today, he let the quiet of the site seep into his spirit. He knew the Lord would hear his concerns and it didn't matter if the land was pristine or natural. Yet something was to be said for the orderly arrangement of the park. It allowed him to focus on the immediate concerns and not the tangled mess of emotions that used to bring him here.

The focus of his emotions now was almost as jumbled.

He was developing a growing interest in his brother's wife. He found himself looking at her, watching her, and each time he did he had to smile. He was not on her glad-to-meet-you list, and he hated that, but he admired her devotion to his dad. Misplaced as it was.

He rubbed his forehead. So much to adjust to. His brother dead before his time and leaving behind a wife and child. Mark was always that rock-steady type, a family man who prided himself on constantly doing the right thing, staying on the path laid out in front of him.

Unlike his younger brother, who was never satisfied, always restless and looking for what lay beyond the trees, over the next hill and down the road ahead. Well, he'd seen it all, done it all and now he was paying the piper. He sucked in a sharp breath as a zinger of pain shot through his thigh. Time for meds and rest, and those exercises he was supposed to do every day.

He needed to remember why he was here. To make peace with Owen. Nothing else mattered.

Chapter Four

Eden set her purse and laptop on the bench inside the back door and headed to the fridge for a drink. It had been a long workday with little accomplished and she was glad to be home. Lucy scurried into the room and wrapped her arms around Eden's waist.

"Hi, Mommy. I missed you today."

Eden scooped her daughter up in her arms. "I always miss you when I'm at work. Did you have fun at school today?"

"Yes. I made you something." She slid to the floor and darted to the sitting area, bringing back a piece of green construction paper. "I made you a macaroni flower. You can hang it on the wall."

Eden's heart melted. The pasta artwork vaguely resembled a flower, but Eden knew Lucy had poured her whole little heart into the project. "It's beautiful, sweetie. I love it. Where should we hang it?"

"On the 'fridgerator so Miss Jackie and Grandpa can see it."

"Good idea."

"I made one for Uncle Blake, too."

Eden froze. "You did? Why?"

"'Cause he needs one on his fridge, don't you think?"

Eden sincerely doubted the man would appreciate the artwork. "I'm sure he does. Well, you can give it to him next time he's here."

"I made him a cane like the one he uses. It's purple."

Eden examined the creation. It looked more realistic than the flower did. She smiled. All that mattered was that Lucy had fun. Eden placed the flower art on the fridge and added a magnet to secure it in place.

Jackie entered the kitchen and beamed at the artwork on the front of the appliance. "I see you got your present."

"Yes, I did. It's beautiful."

She stepped closer and spoke softly. "Did you see the one she made for Blake?"

"Yes." Eden paused. "I saw him pulling out when I got home. Where do you suppose he's going this late?"

"I have no idea. By the way, that was nice of you to loan Blake the truck."

Eden turned away. "Kindness had nothing to do with it. I thought if he had transportation maybe he'd finish his business and be on his way sooner."

"Wow. That doesn't sound like the Eden I know."

Warmth crawled up her neck before her defenses kicked in. "He called Mark a liar."

"What are you talking about?"

"He said I shouldn't believe anything that Mark told me about him."

Jackie inhaled a slow breath. "He's not wrong, you know. Everyone has a bias to something or someone. And the truth is, we all experience things differently.

Mark was always jealous of Blake. He felt he got away with things because he was the youngest."

"I'm sure he did." She could easily see Blake flashing his smile and getting his way.

"And Blake felt Mark was the favorite because he always spent more time with Owen."

Eden hadn't considered his point of view. Maybe she should have. The problem was, which one was true?

Blake slid behind the wheel of the truck Saturday morning and cranked the engine. He was not ready for today. He'd rather stay in bed, or work on Roxy, take another round of physical therapy—anything besides going to the museum and helping Eden.

She wasn't thrilled by the prospect, either. He'd seen the dread in her eyes. Blake honestly had no idea what his father had been thinking when he'd ordered him to assist. No, that wasn't entirely true. Owen wanted his museum and that was that. Though why the old man wanted to start a museum in the first place was beyond him.

Eden's car was in the parking lot when he pulled up at the old church. A small sign pointed the way to the entrance. He turned the knob and stepped inside. "Eden? It's Blake reporting for duty."

He moved farther into the large room, the old fellowship hall, which was now filled with display cases and wall hangings. He frowned. It looked like a sad collection of high school projects.

Eden appeared from the far end of the room along with a welcome aroma.

"Good morning. Is that coffee I smell?"

She nodded and gestured him forward. He followed

her past a room cluttered with boxes and a kitchen before stepping into a small office. Eden waited while he poured his cup and sat down.

"Where do we start? I'm not sure how much help I'll be, though. Not been in many museums. I don't like history."

"I suspected as much."

Her attitude irked him. "But I'm a willing worker and I always finish what I start. So what do we do first?" He smiled but Eden turned away.

"This isn't going to work."

Blake moved to her side. "Of course it will, but I think we need to declare a truce first."

"What do you mean?"

"We need to reach an understanding that while neither of us chose to be here, we'll do our best to finish the project on time for Owen's sake."

She favored him with a skeptical expression. "You think you can do that?"

"Absolutely." He held out his hand. "We have a deal?"

Eden hesitated, but finally slipped her palm against his. The contact created a sensation he'd never experienced before. Not unlike the moment they'd held hands during the blessing. This time, however, he was acutely aware of her delicate fingers, the warmth of her small hand in his and the way it felt as if their hands were meant to be joined. He looked into her eyes and saw them widen. Was she feeling it, too?

Suddenly, she pulled her hand away and touched her neck. "Then you can start by assembling a display." She showed him to the storage room and pointed to a carton. "I assume you know your way around a toolbox."

She met his gaze, her blue eyes icy. "I hope you aren't the type that has to have your hand held every minute."

The image she'd presented bloomed, then quickly wilted in his mind. He focused on her arctic tone. "No, ma'am. No hand-holding necessary."

"Good. You can start with that." The box she indicated was large but narrow.

"What is it?"

"A wall display for large documents and pictures. It has panels that swing back and forth like for posters and such."

Blake looked around the storage room. No space here to work. "Okay if I take it out to the other room?"

"Suit yourself." She went back into her office, leaving him on his own.

So much for working together. He wasn't sure they'd come to an agreement or not. Maybe completing his first task would gain him points.

Leaning the box against the wall, he slit the tape and opened the top. "Whoa." There were at least two million pieces to put together. This might take the rest of the day. If it weren't for his leg, he'd spread it out on the floor, but that wasn't an option. He looked around for a table to use but something familiar caught his attention. The large photo on one wall was of his great-great-grandfather Randolph Sinclair. He'd been a prominent businessman in Blessing and a local congressman. He moved to the next display and the next, then placed his hands on his hips and scanned the room again. "Eden."

She quickly came to his side. "Something wrong?"

He looked at her. "This is all my family stuff. I thought this was supposed to be a museum for Blessing, not the Sinclairs." Some of the color drained from Eden's cheeks.

"Is this all of it?" he continued. "Where's the history of the first way station on the river? The railroad coming through and the timber industry? This looks like the history of Owen Sinclair." When Eden still didn't respond, he turned and faced her. She was staring off into space. "What's going on?"

She met his gaze, her blue eyes clouded. "It's a private museum."

"What does *that* mean? Doesn't this belong to the city?"

She shook her head. "It belongs to Owen alone."

It took only a second for Blake to grasp her true meaning. "Let me guess. This is Owen's private museum so he can show everyone how important the Sinclairs are to the town. He wants to make sure no one forgets their contributions. Right?"

Eden took a long moment to reply. "He feels the family played a big part in the founding and growth of the town."

"They did but so did many other families."

She stiffened. "That's true, but this is Owen's project. He wants to leave a legacy behind for his family."

Blake shook his head. "No, for himself."

"You're wrong. You don't understand."

"Then explain it to me because all I see is re-creation of all the junk in our attic."

"Your dad is passionate about this museum. It's the most important thing in his world at the moment. It gives him a purpose and I'm going to support that in any way possible. I just wish I could have been here more often." She faced him, her eyes shooting daggers.

"And I'm not interested in your opinion. If you don't want to help, then you can leave."

Blake realized he'd let his feelings about his dad cross a line. "No. I'll stay. I shouldn't have said what I did but, I've got to ask, how does the town feel about this?"

"They have strong opinions but it's not up to them. This is a private display. Owen can put anything in here he wants."

"You don't expect anyone to pay to look at this stuff, do you? No one cares about someone else's personal history."

"That's not my concern. I promised to have the museum open for the bicentennial and that's what I'm going to do."

It hit him then that she really loved his father. He didn't understand why, but she did. He smiled and picked up a screwdriver. "Then we'd better get to work."

"Thank you."

The look of relief on her face gave him a twinge of regret. He'd have to watch his words around her. Her loyalty was impressive. He suspected she knew the folly of this project, but she was willing to ignore any negative comments to see Owen's plan fulfilled.

Eden leaned back from her computer and stretched. She'd been writing information cards for the displays, something she'd been putting off. It had given her a reason to stay away from Blake as he worked in the main area. She'd peeked at him a few times, just to make sure he hadn't walked out, but he'd been working diligently each time.

Apparently, he'd inherited the family work ethic

because he hadn't even taken a break. In fact, he'd set up a nice work area for himself. She hadn't considered how his leg might affect his capabilities. Unable to stoop down to do the job, he'd set up a folding table to use as a workbench.

Despite her doubts, Blake might be an asset to the museum after all. As if reading her mind, he suddenly appeared in the office doorway.

"I've got that display thing finished. Where do you want it hung? I may need your help. It's a two-man job."

"Of course." Blake held the frame up to the wall as she gauged the perfect spot. They worked together, her holding, him drilling, until the piece was secure. Then she handed him each frame and he slipped them into the slots.

She hadn't expected him to be so confident about the job. Mark had not been handy around tools or any kind of repair work. Blake, on the other hand, had picked up a variety of useful skills.

"There you go." He swung one of the frames back and forth. "Smooth as butter. Want me to put the pictures inside them?"

She caught herself staring at him. There was a light in his dark eyes that surprised her, as if he really had enjoyed putting the complicated display together. "Uh, no. It's past lunchtime. Are you hungry? The Dixie Deli is just down the way... I could get us some sandwiches." She blanched. Where had that come from? She didn't want to bond with this man. Working together was one thing, but becoming friends was something else.

"I'm starved. You place the order and I'll pick it up."

"No, I'll take care of it. You've worked hard and I'm sure your leg must need rest."

He shrugged. "I won't argue."

Within fifteen minutes, Eden had placed the order and arranged for it to be delivered, and before they knew it, they were seated at the kitchen table unwrapping their sandwiches. They ate in silence for a while.

Blake took a bite of his sandwich and groaned softly. "I'd forgotten how good these were. It's good to know some things stayed the same."

Eden smiled. "The best in town. A new place opened up on Peace Street, but it can't compete." She took a sip of her drink, watching Blake. He'd surprised her today in several ways. "Thank you for your help. That display would have taken me days to put together."

He smiled and nodded. "I figured it would take me that long. But then, I read the instructions." He laughed out loud. "Go figure. No man ever wants to read the instructions. That's the first thing we throw away."

Eden couldn't help but smile. His delight was infectious. "Why is that?"

"Pride, ma'am. Pure pride." He held her gaze, and she thought about the handshake that had started the day. Touching him had been a jolt to her system. As if he'd transferred some of his abundant energy to her through his fingers. His hand had been warm, strong and secure. Like a safe place to stand.

"What's on tap for this afternoon?"

She jerked her thoughts back into line. "Uh, I have a few large documents that can be put into the frames and there's a couple of boxes I need moved around, if you're able."

"I'm ready when you are." He reached for his cane,

which he'd hooked over the back of his chair, but it crashed to the floor. Eden quickly retrieved it, intrigued by the cross carved into the curved handle.

"This is beautiful. I've never seen anything like it."

"Thank you. It's hand carved. One of a kind. A buddy at the rehab center made it for me. He'd give them to anyone who needed one."

She held his gaze, her mind swirling with curiosity. "How long was your recovery?"

"Start to finish, nineteen months. That was between surgeries, and complications and more surgery. The good news is I got to keep my leg."

"It must be hard for you. I mean you were so active and now you're..." Her cheeks heated. She was always blurting out things without thinking.

Blake smiled. "Crippled? Nah. I'm just slowed down a bit, that's all. I can't chase after the bad guys anymore, but I can walk, and in time, I might be able to play golf or hike again."

"So, you'll get better?"

"That's the plan. I'm still doing physical therapy, and I see a chiropractor regularly. Which I need to locate if I'm here long enough." He winked. "Not sure how long my reservation will last."

"I'm sure Jackie will let you stay as long as you need."

He shrugged. "But it's not her house. I'm afraid I may wear out my welcome quickly if my dad has anything to say about it."

Eden turned away. Her warm feelings toward her brother-in-law faded. She couldn't forget what he'd done. "You broke his heart."

"That's a nice explanation. The truth is that Mark

followed his plan. I didn't. That's unforgivable in his eyes."

"Can you blame him? The family business was important to him, and you and Mark were the third generation. It makes sense he'd want to hand his heritage over to his sons. I don't see what's so awful about that."

"Nothing, provided the sons are in agreement. Mark always wanted to work for the company. I didn't."

Eden's defenses rose along with her anger. "Why couldn't you have just done what your father wanted? Why couldn't you set aside your own selfish desire for his sake?"

Blake held her gaze, his eyes hard and angry. She hadn't meant to upset him, but she refused to feel guilty about her position.

His jaw flexed. "Why couldn't he set aside his selfish desire and allow his son to live his own life?"

Eden placed her fingertips on her temple. He'd countered her assault with the truth. "I'm sorry. I just thought if you'd been here to help, then none of this would have happened."

Blake met her gaze. "None of what would have happened. The museum?"

"Yes. No. I mean, Mark's stress trying to save the company, Dad's heart attack. All of it."

"What do you mean *save the company*?" he demanded.

"It was in trouble. Something happened, I never knew what, but Mark was desperate, almost frantic to turn things around. But he couldn't. We had no idea at the time he was sick."

"Sick. What do you mean?" Blake leaned forward, his dark eyes probing. "How did my brother die?"

"Mark had a brain tumor."

"He didn't tell you about the cancer?"

She shook her head. "He complained of headaches, then he started becoming short-tempered, easily aggravated and angry over the smallest things. I thought it was the stress of the job. Then he started to withdraw, keeping to himself and spending more time at the office. Some days I wouldn't see him at all, and when he did come home, he'd sleep in the spare room. I tried to get him to see a doctor, but he'd only get angrier." She tugged at her collar. "I thought he was having an affair. I didn't recognize my husband any longer. Things had gotten so bad, so volatile, I couldn't allow Lucy to live in that environment, so I contacted an attorney to begin divorce proceedings."

"Was the tumor to blame?"

She nodded. "We only found out after his death. The doctor said it wasn't uncommon for the tumor to cause significant changes in personality. Some patients can even experience delusions." What would Blake say if she told him the whole truth, about the gambling habit, losing all their savings and investments, the house and life insurance?

"Where was Owen during this?"

"He'd retired several years earlier. He had supreme confidence in Mark. He used to brag about how well his son was doing, and how he was taking the company in a new direction."

"What about now? Is the company still struggling?"

She shrugged. "I think so."

"Then why isn't Dad back at work?"

Eden took a long moment to reply. "He did at first. Then two months later, he had his heart attack. After that he stopped caring about anything. Until he got the idea to start his museum. That gave him a focus, and he threw himself into the project. And he enlisted me to spearhead it."

"Despite your full-time job?"

Eden nodded. "I couldn't refuse him. He was struggling and this was the only thing that gave him hope, that he got up for each morning."

"Who's running the company?"

"Norman Young."

"I know him. Good man." Blake leaned forward and laid his hand on her forearm. "Well, I'm here now. You don't have to do all this alone. We're a team. Okay?"

Eden told herself to remove her arm but she didn't. There was comfort in his touch, and his words. She realized how much she'd needed help and encouragement. She'd been battling alone for a long time. But she hadn't expected help to come from her bad-boy brother-in-law. *He's a charmer.* Her husband's words flashed in her mind, and she pulled her arm from his touch. Time to turn the tables. "Now can I ask you a question?"

"Shoot."

"All this time, you didn't call or let anyone know where you were. The family needed you. The company took every ounce of energy Mark and Owen had. They could have used your help." She heard the accusation in her tone and took a deep breath to calm down. She looked at Blake. "I suppose you never thought about the family, did you?"

He toyed with his drink, avoiding her gaze. "At first, I thought about calling, but the truth was, I didn't want to know what was going on. Then after a while it was easier to not think about life back here."

She pressed her lips together. "Mark told me how you were always disrupting things, wanting the attention, getting him into one mess after another."

Blake studied her a long moment. "Is that how he remembered it?"

Her defenses kicked in. Was he calling her husband a liar again? "Why couldn't you have just done what your father asked and joined the company? Would that have been so difficult?"

Blake held her gaze. "Yes. I had no choice. After Mom died, I couldn't stay here. I had a life of my own to live. Not the one Dad had mapped out."

She squared her shoulders to regain her composure. They would never see things the same way so it was futile to keep rehashing everything. "Well, I appreciate your help…"

"You're welcome." He stood, gripping his cane. "Point me to the next project, Madam Curator."

Eden kept her expression neutral but inside she smiled at his levity. Maybe working with Blake wouldn't be so bad after all.

Or was she slowly succumbing to his charm?

Chapter Five

Blake eased open the back door to the kitchen early Sunday morning and glanced around. No one here yet. He made his way to the coffeepot and poured a cup. For some reason, the coffee here in the main house tasted better than what he could make in the studio. Today he felt like taking a chance on seeing family. So far so good. He turned and stopped in his tracks as Lucy, Cuddles and Eden entered the room. His niece and her dog stopped at his feet. However, Eden halted and turned away.

"Good morning, Lucy. How are you and Cuddles today?"

"Good. It's Sunday school day."

"Do you like Sunday school?"

Lucy nodded vigorously. "We sing songs and color and do finger plays. Watch." She entwined her little fingers into a fist. "It's the church and the people are inside." He chuckled as she tried to duplicate the old finger play. She stole his heart every time he saw her.

Eden placed a bowl on the table. "Lucy, eat your cereal, please."

Owen came into the kitchen and Blake sensed a sudden drop in the temperature. His dad always could bring a chill with his presence. Owen stopped at the coffee maker, his back to them as he spoke.

"You're still here." He turned and glared at Blake.

Blake fought back his emotions. "I am." Not a good start to the day. He debated whether to stay and irritate his dad or go and leave the rest of the family in peace.

"Morning, everyone." Jackie breezed into the room. "Y'all need to shake a leg or we'll be late for church."

Blake spoke without thinking. "Would you mind if I came along?"

Jackie gave him a broad smile. "We'd be delighted."

"Thanks. It's been a few weeks. I could use some spiritual fortification." He set his cup on the counter and took his cane. "I'll go change and meet you there."

Jackie gave him a hug and whispered in his ear, "I think your dad is coming around."

Blake highly doubted that, judging from the scowl on his parent's face. He nodded but his stomach was doing flip-flops. He'd greatly underestimated the depth of his father's response to his return.

Attendance at church was exactly what he needed, and he hoped Pastor Miller gave one of those sermons that felt like it was directed at him personally.

Blake waited until the family had driven off before sliding behind the wheel of the truck. Attending the same church service as his family was one thing, sitting with them was a different story. There was no way he could share a pew with his dad. That would only create tension for everyone and that was the last thing they needed. There was enough of that swirling around at home.

Blake managed to enter the church without having to speak to anyone and took a seat in the back row of the sanctuary. He searched for Eden and found her sitting toward the front next to Jackie. Owen was on Jackie's other side. Lucy must be at children's church.

A touch of envy settled in his chest. It would have been nice to sit with his family, but he had a feeling that was a wish that would never come true. Owen Sinclair was a hard, stubborn man who never admitted to being wrong.

Blake paid only scant attention to the first part of the service. The music swirled around him, but his thoughts were settled on the conversation he'd had with Eden yesterday at the museum.

As if the family dynamic wasn't complicated enough, he'd learned that his brother had endured cancer alone. His tumor had put his marriage at risk, and something had happened at the Sinclair Properties office that had put the business at risk.

Hearing Eden talk about Mark's change in personality, isolating himself from everyone, and his frantic behavior at the office, left Blake more conflicted than ever. Mark had been more like their father than he'd understood. The workaholic nature and the pride that refused to ask for help were all traits that Owen had displayed daily.

His gaze sought out Eden again, a knot of resentment forming in his chest at the way she'd been treated over the last few years. Mark's selfish approach to his illness honestly made his blood boil. A husband and wife were to stand alongside one another and share the burdens for better or worse. And the way Owen had further burdened Eden by putting her in charge of his pet project when she was already spread thin with her regular job and raising Lucy was outrageous. Not to mention helping Jackie with his self-centered father. He wanted to rescue her from it all and take her someplace safe, where she could find a little peace. She deserved that. And more.

But it wasn't his place to provide her with any of that. Blake pinched the bridge of his nose, then trained his gaze on the pulpit. Eden was starting to get under his skin. He thought about her constantly. It was a dangerous habit to start. She was his brother's widow. Off-limits. Out of bounds.

He'd come home to make amends. Falling for his sister-in-law would be the ultimate sin.

Pastor Miller stepped to the pulpit and Blake set aside everything but the words he was about to hear. It was time to worship, not worry. As he hoped, Pastor Miller's sermon hit home.

The benediction was spoken, and the pastor made his way to the door to greet people as they left. Blake intended to slip out unnoticed, but the reverend stepped forward and caught his attention.

"Good to see you here, Blake. Not sitting with your family?"

He grinned wryly. "Things haven't come to that yet."

"I understand. Come see me this week. We'll pick up our conversation where we left off the other day." He glanced at the cane. "You still have to tell me about your adventures."

"I'll be there."

Blake returned to the house ahead of the family and changed into jeans and a T-shirt. The weather was as close to perfect as you could ask for on a Sunday. Sunshine, warm gentle breezes and azaleas budding out gave a man's spirits a lift. He had no plans today but to sit here on the porch and soak it all in.

"Uncle Blake! What ya doing?"

He smiled as Lucy came toward him at full gallop, ponytail bobbing. She looked cute in little jeans and a shirt with a glittery flower on the front. "I'm just enjoying the nice day. What are you doing?"

"Visiting you. I brought you a present. I made it at school. You can put it in your house."

Blake took the construction paper and chuckled as he recognized the image of his cane executed in macaroni.

"Wow. This is beautiful. Did you do this all by yourself?"

Lucy grinned and nodded. "Yep. I'm good at art. Where you gonna put it?"

Blake stifled a laugh and rubbed his chin. "Well, how about on the fridge? No, that's too ordinary. It needs to be someplace special. How about in the living room where I can see it all the time? And I'll take a picture of it for my phone, then whenever I think about you I can look at my cane picture."

Lucy nodded. "Yes. I like it."

She reached for the handrail on the steps leading to the porch but instead of taking them she swung around to the opposite side and inched up along the narrow border. "Be careful there. Don't fall."

"I won't." She gave him a big smile. "I do this all the time." At the top of the steps, she transferred her feet to the outside of the porch rail and continued along the edge. "This is my trick. No one else can do this."

Blake watched her closely, hoping she wouldn't fall

because with his leg, there was no way he could get to her quickly. Thankfully, the porch was only a foot and a half off the ground. "How long did it take you to learn this amazing trick?"

Lucy shrugged, then let go and jumped down to the ground. She turned, smiled and threw her arms in the air. "Ta-da."

Blake laughed and clapped his hands. "Very good."

She hurried up the steps and came to his side. "I like climbing. You want to play with me?"

How could he refuse this adorable child? "Sure. What are we going to play? Tea party, dolls, dress-up?"

Lucy scrunched up her face. "No. I want to play ball. I'll go get it."

She scurried off, disappearing around the side of the house, then reappearing with a small soccer ball. "See. It's pink and purple. 'Cause it's a girl's ball."

"Of course it is. Well, Lucy, I can kick the ball with one foot but not the other, if that's okay."

He joined her on the lawn. He kept his cane with him. The ground could be uneven. "Are you ready?"

She stared at him. "Do you have a boo-boo?"

"Yep. A big one."

"Is that why you walk funny?"

Blake nodded and held his leg out. "It won't bend."

"Oh." Curiosity satisfied, the little girl set the ball down and kicked it. He sent it right back to her and she giggled. "You kick better than Jeffery."

"Who's Jeffery?"

Lucy made a sour face. "A boy at school. He kicks like a girl."

"I'll take that as a compliment of the utmost significance."

Blake could easily lose his heart to this child. An ache had begun inside him, wrapped in envy and pierced with hopelessness. His brother had been a fortunate man. Had Mark fully appreciated his family? Having a lovely wife and sweet little girl like Lucy would be all that he'd ask for. It wasn't in the cards for him, though.

He doubted it ever would be.

Eden looked up from her laptop when Owen entered the kitchen and went to stand at the window. He was unusually quiet since they'd come home from church, almost thoughtful, which was out of character for him. "Can I get you a drink or something to snack on?"

"No." He clasped his hands behind his back and continued to stare outside. Curious, she rose and went to his side. Lucy and Blake were kicking the soccer ball in the yard. Lucy was bubbling with energy and from the big smile on her brother-in-law's face, he was having fun, too.

He had a great smile. She winced at that thought. Not that it mattered.

"She's like him."

Eden looked at Owen. "Yes, she resembles Mark in many ways."

"He was always moving. Always active. Never could sit still."

She realized he was talking about Blake. She looked at the pair in the yard. They were thoroughly enjoying each other. Despite his bad leg, Blake was moving well. Was her daughter really like her uncle? The thought was both disturbing and oddly comforting.

"He was a climber, too."

Eden's throat tightened. She'd tried to curb Lucy's desire to climb anything in sight but with no success. She studied Owen more closely. What was he saying? That Lucy would turn out to be a rebel like her uncle? Her heart skipped a beat. Though Blake actually turned out to be an honorable man. Perhaps Owen didn't know. "He was a detective wounded in the line of duty."

Owen worked his jaw. "Reckless fool." He turned and abruptly left the kitchen. What had he seen that had prompted those observations? There'd been no bitterness in his voice, just a statement of fact.

Her text alert sounded, and she hurried to pick up her phone and quickly scanned the message from her boss, Virginia Thomas, director of the South Mississippi Preservation Society.

Mrs. Langley has given us permission to photograph Beaumont. She'll meet you there tomorrow with the key.

Eden started to type a reply but dialed her boss's number instead. "Hi, Virginia. This is great news. What do you suppose changed their minds?"

"I have no idea. Honestly. It shouldn't be this difficult to decide whether to sell us the house or not."

"True, but when you're dealing with six heirs, living in five different states, the first thing to go is communication." The bickering had been going on ever since the owner, Mrs. Vincent Harper, had passed and left the home to her distant nieces and nephews.

"If you ask me, it's all about greed. The heirs know that property is worth more if they doze the house and sell it to a developer for retail space. They could make millions."

Eden chewed her lower lip. "Maybe granting us permission to take pictures is a step in a positive direction. At least we'll have documentation, if nothing else. If we could just find the key to getting that Ohio heir to change his mind... Everyone else is on board. At least they were at the last teleconference."

"Their lawyer is pushing for a settlement. Everyone wants a payday."

Eden couldn't disagree. The society had tried everything to convince them of the importance of the nearly three-hundred-year-old structure. However, the nephew in Sandusky, Ohio, wasn't budging. As a real estate broker, he knew the land on which Beaumont sat was worth a small fortune today, and he was determined to get as much money as possible.

"Thank you for letting me know. I'll be at Beaumont first thing tomorrow."

"Oh, I meant to ask, did you ever find someone to help you at the museum?"

Eden took a moment to measure her words. "Yes. Owen ordered Blake to help me."

"Blake? The prodigal brother-in-law? How are you going to work with that man every day?"

A twinge of regret skittered through Eden's mind. She'd unfairly talked Blake down to her boss. "He actually started yesterday, and he was very helpful. He's not what I expected. He likes dogs." She wasn't sure where that thought came from, except he'd made friends with Cuddles, who now treated him like a long-lost friend.

"Well, will wonders never cease."

After the call ended, Eden opened her home page

and looked at the image of Beaumont that served as her wallpaper. She wasn't sure why, but the old home had become special to her. She'd worked on several other historic homes in Blessing, but Beaumont had touched her soul. It would break her heart if the society lost the home, though she was beginning to think that was inevitable. She knew the heirs would likely sell it and the new owners would bring in an excavator and demolish it, destroying centuries of history in the process.

Why couldn't people see the value in preserving the past?

Eden and Lucy entered the kitchen the next morning to find Blake sitting at the breakfast table. She hadn't seen her brother-in-law since yesterday. He'd come to church alone and apparently sat in the back. She'd caught sight of him speaking with Pastor Miller at the end of the service. Why hadn't he sat with the family? Probably because of Owen. It would have been uncomfortable for them all.

"Uncle Blake. I'm happy to see you."

Blake lifted Lucy onto his lap and smiled as his niece gave his neck a big hug. "I'm happy to see you, too."

"Are you going to make baby pancakes for us?"

Blake chuckled and glanced at Eden with his eyebrows raised. "I don't know. Are we?"

"Sorry, Lucy. Not this morning. Mommy has an appointment and you need to get to school early today for the field trip to the library. I'll fix you a muffin and a glass of milk."

Blake joined her at the sink, rinsing his cup and setting it aside. "Do you want me to go to the museum and start on those boxes in the storage room?"

"No. I'll need to be there as we go through them. You have the day off. I'm meeting someone this morning, so we'll have to postpone that for now."

She glanced at her watch a few minutes later. "Lucy, are you almost finished? I have to be at Beaumont on time, so we need to get moving."

"Yes, Mommy. I'm done."

Blake moved to the table and picked up after Lucy. "Beaumont. Is that the old rickety hodgepodge place out on Thompson Road?"

Eden bristled at his assessment of the historic home. "It's not a hodgepodge. It's a perfect compilation of the history of Blessing."

He grimaced. "If you say so. When we were kids it was always the place you toilet-papered because it was so ugly."

"Stop! It's not ugly… It's unique. And it's rich with history."

"Why are you going out there?"

"I'm meeting one of the heirs. A Mrs. Barbara Langley. She's given us access to the home to take pictures." She quickly explained the situation to him. "We may not acquire the house, but at least I'll have archival evidence of every nook and cranny for future reference."

Blake held her gaze a long moment. "That old place is important to you, isn't it?"

"It's important to *Blessing*. Lucy, get your backpack."

"Mind if I tag along?"

Eden spun around and stared. "To the house? Why?"

Blake grinned and shrugged. "Why not? I'm free and it's a big place. You might need some company."

She didn't have time to discuss the issue. "Suit yourself. Just don't get in my way."

"No, ma'am. I'll try not to."

She picked up her purse. "I have to drop Lucy off at school on the way."

A short while later, Eden pulled into the end of the long winding drive leading to the Beaumont Plantation. She would never say it out loud, but Blake wasn't entirely wrong about the place. While historically a treasure trove of Blessing history, aesthetically it was a hodgepodge of periods and styles.

Perched on the edge of a deep ravine above the river below, the original rustic building had been a way station and inn during the 1780s and was one of the earliest structures in the area. Its low-pitched roof shielded a wide porch with hand-hewn rails and posts. Attached to the east end of the small building was a two-story brick Federal addition complete with portico and Doric columns.

The addition on the west end, added in 1858, was a three-story Greek Revival. The formal structure had become the front of the home, complete with Corinthian columns and double galleries. Each section had been designed according to current trends and requirements of the time.

Eden couldn't explain her affection for the old home. But it was the embodiment of three centuries of history and she wanted to see it preserved and not bulldozed for another apartment or retail complex.

Blake leaned forward and peered out of the windshield as Eden pulled to a stop near the middle of the sprawling home. "It hasn't changed. Maybe a bit shabbier than I remember."

She shot him a scowl. "It's been empty for two years. What did you expect?"

Another car pulled up and a woman got out. Eden greeted her warmly. "Thank you so much for allowing me access. The society really appreciates this."

"I'm glad to help. I'm on your side. I would love to sell the home to the society and see it preserved the way it deserves. But I'm afraid most of my cousins have no heart for anything old and only see dollar signs."

"I know. It'll break my heart to see the home destroyed." Eden sensed Blake slowly approaching. She turned and saw him waiting patiently with his hands in his pockets. He looked relaxed and at ease. It occurred to her that Mark had never looked that way. "Uh, Mrs. Langley, this is Blake Sinclair, my...brother-in-law."

They chatted a few moments, then the woman left, and Eden held up the keys. "Finally, I get to examine this place inch by inch."

"How 'bout I leave you here and come back when you're done?"

One look at his expression and she realized he was joking. "Oh no. You asked to come along. You have to stick it out."

She smiled as she hurried up to the door in the oldest section of the home. Her heart beat quickly with anticipation. Today was better than a birthday. Inserting the large key into the lock, she turned it. Nothing happened. She tried several more times with no success. Blake reached over and took the keys from her hand, brushing against her fingers and sending an electric jolt through her system. She kept her eyes averted for fear of him seeing her reaction. Eden thought she heard him clear his throat.

"Maybe it just needs a firmer hand." He inserted the large key and was rewarded with a sound snap. The knob turned and the wide, thick door swung open. Blake smiled and gestured her to enter.

She did so quickly, moving ahead of him to find space to breathe. That proved harder to do than expected. The air inside was stale and musty. She coughed. Blake did likewise.

"I don't suppose we can open a window?"

"No, but we can leave the doors open." She pointed to the door on the opposite end of the long entry room. "We can get a little cross-ventilation."

Blake saw to the door while Eden retrieved her camera.

"So where do we start?" He gestured with his hands. "The old section, the older section or the *really* old section." He smiled but Eden only scowled and turned her back, focusing on the long dark room.

"Why don't you see if you can find lights? I know the house has electricity. Mrs. Langley arranged for it to be turned on today."

By the time Blake returned, Eden had completed her inventory of the center room, and its side rooms, snapping photos as she went.

Blake approached her, brushing dust and cobwebs from his head and shoulders. "Sorry. It took a while to locate the fuse box. It was in the cellar underneath the back portion of the house."

She smiled. "I should have told you to wear old clothes." She opened the door to the brick Federal structure at the rear. Blake followed, bumping into her when she stopped to snap an overall shot of the first room. She turned and frowned. "You don't have to stick to me like glue. Go wander around or something. This is going to take a while."

Blake looked at her in disbelief. "Are you kidding? This place is huge and we're all alone. This whole house is a disaster waiting to happen. Rotten floors, crumbling ceilings—even the furniture looks like it would collapse if you sat on it. No. I'm not leaving your side."

A slow rising heat moved through Eden's body. He was being protective. Willing to be bored for several hours just to make sure she was safe. She looked away. No one had ever cared enough about her interests to stand by her. Not even Mark. He never understood her love of history and her passion for saving old buildings.

"I'll try not to take too long."

Blake shrugged and flashed her a smile. "No rush. Indulge yourself."

Eden studied him a moment. Blake was a completely different man from what she'd expected. He continually surprised her with his thoughtful gestures. It was getting harder to maintain her old image of him. An image she'd pasted together from bits and pieces she'd heard from Mark and Owen. It was unsettling to think that they were wrong, and the prodigal might have been the victim all along.

Free to concentrate on her work, Eden captured photos of every detail of the Federal section of the house, shocked to discover that it had been over an hour since she'd checked in with Blake. He'd followed her upstairs earlier, then took a seat on a sturdy-looking ottoman in the upper hall.

She hurried back. He was still there, staring at his cell phone. He grinned and slipped it into the back pocket of his faded jeans. The pale blue V-neck sweater he wore drew attention to his dark brown eyes. She swallowed. "Sorry. I forgot about you."

Blake chuckled. "That means you're having a good time. Where to now?"

"The Greek Revival addition. It's in the best shape."

They made their way downstairs and headed toward the front of the house. "Mrs. Harper lived in this part. She used the front parlor and kitchen and main bedroom upstairs." She looked around. "I can't imagine living here all alone. It's sad. All these beautiful old antiques and paintings but no one to share them with."

Blake looked skeptical. "This whole house is sad, if you ask me."

"I disagree. It's filled with stories, family dramas and happy times, from the 1700s to today. It may not have the beauty of some of the old Natchez homes like Dunleith or Longwood, but it has more stories to tell." She reached out and touched an old hall table. "And it's been owned by succeeding generations of the same family. A family with deep roots."

They walked into the front foyer of the house and Blake uttered a grunt of approval. "This at least looks like an antebellum mansion. What will happen to all this furniture and the crystal chandeliers?"

"The heirs will probably hold an auction. There's a lot of history sitting in these rooms. These furnishings are fine examples of Empire and Rococo Revival styles." She set her bag and camera on a petticoat table. And brushed a stray strand of hair from her cheek.

Blake smiled at her. "Are you thirsty? What say we

run to the store and get a drink and bite to eat, then come back."

She shook her head. "No need. I have water in the car. And if you like applesauce and yogurt in a pouch, we can use some of the stash I keep on hand for Lucy." Blake's skeptical expression made her chuckle.

"A pouch? That's a new one."

She returned his grin. He was making this task more enjoyable than she'd ever imagined. "Stick around long enough and you'll learn all kinds of new things."

His smile shifted and his eyes narrowed slightly. "I'm looking forward to that."

Oddly enough, so was she.

Chapter Six

Blake carried the remnants of their snack back to the car, then turned to look at the sprawling ancient house. For whatever reason, Eden loved this shabby old place. He didn't understand it, but he liked watching her enjoy it. She was dressed in a bright blue sweater and faded jeans, looking like a spring flower in the middle of winter. He swallowed and coughed. He shouldn't be noticing his brother's wife. Widow.

Back inside, he found her in the formal parlor, looking at her phone. She turned to him and his heart jumped sideways in his chest. Her cheeks were rosy, her blue eyes sparkled with joy and her smile stole his breath. She was the most beautiful woman he'd ever met. It took him a long moment to regain his composure.

"So, what do you think now about my house?"

His eyebrows rose. "*Your* house?"

"Wishful thinking, I suppose." She shrugged. "But I really love it. If only I could afford to buy it and bring it back to its former glory."

Blake emitted a long whistle. "That would take a huge amount of capital."

Eden sighed. "Go ahead and be practical. But a girl can dream, right? I'd love to own an old home someday."

He came and sat beside her on the small settee. The wistful tone in her voice made him curious. "What is it about this place, other than the history, that intrigues you so much?"

"I don't know. Maybe because it's neglected, unappreciated. It's a little cottage that managed to hang on through three centuries and grew into a mansion. Changing and adapting. The three disjointed sections stuck together over time, making a home for several generations."

"Do you feel disjointed or neglected?"

She met his gaze, then quickly picked up her camera and stood. "I need to finish up."

Blake followed, gently taking her arm. "Eden, did Mark neglect you and Lucy?"

She jerked from his grasp. "You have no right to ask such a thing. You don't know anything about my husband, or our relationship, just like you don't know anything about Owen and his life."

She marched off across the wide hall and into the room on the other side of the house. He decided it was best to keep his distance for the time being. He'd obviously hit a nerve. His own nerves were vibrating, too. Had his brother neglected his family? Had things between Mark and Eden been worse than she'd let on? He made a mental note to seek out Jackie and ask some questions.

Blake waited for Eden to finish downstairs, but it was obvious she was taking extra time and keeping her distance. He took the broad curving staircase to the second floor and the wide upper hallway. The double doors leading to the second-story gallery beckoned him. He turned the knobs and stepped through the double doors and walked to the railing. "Wow. I could get used to this view. These live oaks are unreal," he mused out loud, drinking in the sight. "This must be one of the highest points in Blessing."

Footsteps alerted him to Eden's presence. He heard her moving about in the bedrooms. When the click of the camera sounded from the upper hall, he turned and looked at her. She was taking pictures from the doorway. "You'll get some great shots out here."

"I can get all I need from here."

"But you can't appreciate the view from there." He motioned her to join him but she stood still as if frozen. She'd gone pale, her eyes wide with fear. Realization hit him like a blow. "Eden, are you afraid of heights?"

"No. Yes. Maybe."

Slowly he walked toward her and stretched out his hand for the camera. "I'll do it." He could see she was shaking. "Tell me what you want."

It took her a moment to speak. "The moldings, railing…" She made a sweeping gesture. "All of it."

Blake took snapshots of everything he could imagine she would want, then started back to the open door. Eden had moved back four or five feet from the opening. He returned the camera, studying her closely. "Are you all right?"

"I'm fine." She turned and started for the stairs, hurrying down them and disappearing down the center hallway.

He found her standing beside the car and he decided

to let his curiosity linger awhile and not press her for an explanation.

"Ready to go?"

She stared at the camera a moment. "I need a few more shots if you don't mind."

He couldn't imagine what they'd missed. They'd captured the entire house and the outbuildings. "Okay. Where to now?"

She handed him the camera. "Would you go around to the back side of the house and take pictures?"

Odd request. "Sure, but why don't you— Oh." The back of Beaumont ran along the deep ravine. The last place she'd want to go if she was afraid of heights. He smiled. "I'll be back in a flash."

A short time later, he returned. "Mission accomplished." Back in the car, they drove home in silence. Blake fought hard not to press for answers. She was so strong and capable. Where had the fear come from? She sighed heavily and glanced at him.

"My parents were killed when I was six. I was ten when my foster mother took several of us to a carnival, and we rode the Ferris wheel. We were at the very top when it got stuck. We were there for over an hour while they fixed the problem. But it was windy that day and the car kept swinging. After that, I didn't want to be anywhere too far from the ground."

"I don't blame you."

She gave him a skeptical glance. "Go ahead. Say it."

"Say what?"

"What everyone says when they learn about my phobia. It's all in my head. There's nothing to be afraid of. Don't be such a scaredy-cat. The teasing and scolding would go on forever."

"Nah. I wouldn't do that. We can't help what we're afraid of." The look of gratitude in her blue eyes brought warmth to his veins.

"I suppose you're not afraid of anything. Being a big, brave policeman and all."

Blake chuckled. "Oh, I'm afraid of plenty of things. Snakes, quicksand, monsters from outer space. My dad…"

Eden giggled. "Which one is the scariest?"

Blake considered his reply. He wanted to tell her the truth. "I'm afraid of being alone the rest of my life."

Eden froze, her hands tight on the steering wheel. "We're all afraid of that."

He stole quick little glances at her on the way home. She'd always given him the impression she was content, that Mark had been the perfect husband. Now he was beginning to wonder if Eden was keeping part of herself hidden and putting on a confident mask to face the world.

Or was he just a man who was attracted to a lovely woman and wanted to know all about her? Either way, he needed to take a step back. Because he could quite literally be stepping into emotional quicksand with no way out.

Eden parked the car near the garage and waited as Blake climbed out. "Thank you for going with me."

"Anytime. You going to look at all your pictures now?"

"No. I have to go to the office for the rest of the day. Virginia will want to know how it went today."

She watched him walk slowly toward the studio leaning on his cane. The time at Beaumont must have taxed his bad leg. She regretted that but she was very grateful for his help this morning. Turning the car around, Eden started for work.

"Did Mark neglect you?"

Her throat closed up. The question had thrown her for a loop. Why had he asked that question? What had she said or done that might have tipped him off? Mark hadn't meant to neglect his family. He hadn't intentionally destroyed their life. He'd been sick… It was out of his control. Tears stung her eyes. Even so, the truth of his question hit home. Mark had neglected them in a way, working long hours, missing events and time with Lucy. She'd never said anything, never allowed herself to acknowledge that she felt obligated to maintain the image of perfection Owen always placed around her husband.

Mark wasn't perfect. She'd loved him dearly, but it had always felt one-sided. Suddenly, a spark of anger coursed through her. She was his wife. Mother of his child. How dare Blake expose these feelings!

Her hands gripped the steering wheel. Why didn't Mark tell anyone he was ill? Why didn't he ask for help? She could have made his remaining time special, meaningful. But he'd chosen to go it alone, turn his back on everyone and everything.

The same way Blake had done. A sobering thought.

Guilt boiled in her chest. What was wrong with her? Mark had *cancer*. He couldn't help what happened. It's not like he deliberately ignored her or planned to lose everything they'd worked for.

Oh, but how she craved the support and understanding Blake had given her today. But it was wrong. So wrong. She could never have feelings for her renegade brother-in-law. What did that say about her own flawed nature?

Was she so lonely that she'd accept attention from a man who walked away from his family? She wished, at this moment, that Blake would choose to walk away again.

Blake fixed a sandwich and a drink and sat down at the small table in the studio. His mind wasn't on his lunch but on the morning at Beaumont with Eden. He'd asked to go along on a whim, having nothing lined up for the rest of the day. But he'd discovered a new side to his brother's widow. So far, he'd experienced her compassion, her devotion and her love of family. Today he'd been introduced to her tender heart.

Eden possessed a deep affection for the old, run-down plantation house. He wasn't surprised since she did work for the Preservation Society, but he was curious about the significance of the old house in her life. Her comments about neglect and being disjointed held a deeper meaning. She'd denied she'd felt those things personally, but he was beginning to think there was more to the story. He wondered if it might have something to do with being orphaned at a young age. She'd connected with the place for some psychological reason, and he wanted to know what it was.

In the meantime, he'd try to help out by continuing to work at the museum. There were still a couple of furniture pieces to assemble. Provided he could get his dad to give him a key.

He headed to the house, praying his old man was in a cooperative mood. Owen was seated in his favorite chair in the family room watching golf on TV. He looked at Blake briefly, then looked away. "What do you want?"

"A key to the museum. Eden isn't there today, so I thought I'd keep working. There are a lot of boxes to unpack still."

Owen didn't look at him but gestured toward the back of the house. "There's a spare on the key rack in the kitchen. Take care with those items. They're valuable."

Blake set his jaw. "Important *Sinclair* things, you mean."

"Watch your tone. The Sinclair name is respected here in Blessing."

Blake tried to rein in his anger. "So are the names of Tierney, Kovak, Jackson and Summerville. They have all contributed to the town."

Owen snorted. "Hardly the same thing."

He took a moment to calm himself. There was no use trying to open his father's eyes. They were blind to everything but his own point of view, but Blake could at least try to help his sister-in-law. "You do realize that Eden has a full-time job, and a child to care for. Do you think it's fair to put the burden of the museum all on her shoulders?"

"Eden is more than capable. And willing. She does as she's asked, unlike other members of the family."

The selfishness of the man had no end. "You mean she follows your orders? You have no right to stress her out this way."

"And you have no right to question my decisions."

Clenching his jaw, Blake turned and walked out. Some things never changed. He needed time to regain his equilibrium. Something to keep his hands busy. It was the only thing that helped.

Time to work on Roxy.

Chapter Seven

Eden scrolled through the photos she'd taken at Beaumont. As she did so, her emotions were pulled between delight and gratitude for having a detailed catalog of the historic home, and sadness that, in all likelihood, the house would be demolished, and all this architectural evidence would be lost.

Her gaze drifted to the sitting room window and the studio at the far end of the east wing of Oakley Hall. If someone had told her a week ago that she would enjoy time with her brother-in-law, she would have scoffed. But she had. Blake had been the perfect companion. He hadn't talked too much, hadn't made her feel rushed and, most importantly, hadn't made any snide comments about her love of the old place. As a result, she'd come away with more photos than she'd ever expected.

It had been several days since she'd toured Beaumont with Blake. She hadn't seen much of him since then. He'd kept to himself, presumably working in the barn on his beloved motorcycle. Just as well. She had left that day with a mound of confusing emotions and thoughts. Blake Sinclair wasn't what she'd expected.

She tapped a key on her laptop and scanned the next set of pictures. Blake's image appeared. She hadn't intentionally taken his picture, but somehow, he'd managed to insert himself into several. She leaned forward and looked closer at the one with him in the yard when they'd gone to the car for a snack.

Blake was standing with one foot on the lower step of the original house. He was looking over his shoulder and his expression was one of amusement. She was struck once again by the difference between her husband and his brother. Blake wore jeans and a V-neck sweater with the sleeves pushed up, exposing his strong forearms.

He looked comfortable, relaxed, the way he always did when he played soccer with Lucy.

In all their years of marriage, she couldn't recall Mark even owning a pair of jeans. His casual dress consisted of khaki slacks and a polo shirt. He was always conscious of his position in the town. Looking anything less than presentable was not his way.

Eden couldn't help but wonder, if her husband had been more willing to shed his work persona, if they might have had more family fun together. But Mark was never willing to let his hair down. Not even with Lucy.

A wave of guilt shot through her like lightning. What was she thinking? She had no business comparing Mark with his brother. The two men bore no resemblance to one another in any way. Blake might not be the man she'd expected him to be, but that didn't elevate him to the level of her husband.

Eden chewed her lip. So why was she having nightmares again after all these years? They all had the same theme and involved a shadowy figure approaching her in the dark. She'd turn to run away but her feet were made of lead. She'd come awake, breathing hard and sweating, and filled with a sense of impending doom.

The dreams had started up again when Blake had come home. Closing her laptop, she reached for her purse and her keys. She needed time away from Oakley Hall and the museum. She needed to find a quiet, peaceful place to think and find some answers.

She needed to visit the bridge.

There was only one car in the parking lot when she arrived at the Blessing Bridge Prayer Garden. She hoped the person was secluded away in a quiet spot. She needed alone time to work through her emotions. It had been several months since she'd come here and laid her fears and worries at the foot of the cross. During Mark's last year, she felt as if she'd worn a trench from the parking lot to the bridge, she'd been here so often.

At the apex of the arched bridge, Eden stopped and let her gaze drift around the lovely landscaped grounds. Spring flowers were emerging, azaleas budding out, making the area bright with color.

Color was the thing she was missing in her life. With the exception of Lucy, who was like a ray of sweet sunshine. Her daughter was her whole life now. But the joy and exuberance had been missing for a long time, replaced by worry, obligations and responsibility. The last time she'd had fun was...

The morning at Beaumont with Blake.

Guilt washed through her once again, and she bowed her head. Her prayer rose in a flurry of appeals, confessions and supplications. Her emotions were a mishmash of feelings and she blamed Blake's return for her disjointed state. His presence here was disturbing her predictable routine and ramping up her worry for her father-in-law. The four of them, Owen, Jackie, Lucy and her, had a comfortable life. Blake threatened it all.

She'd found a measure of peace over Mark's death and his decision to keep his cancer from his family. Only afterward she'd learned that the tumor in his brain had been the cause of his personality change and erratic behavior. She was still working through the anger over his destroying their future, but her anger was always followed by the reminder that Mark had been ill. He hadn't deliberately lost their money. He wasn't himself. At least that's what the doctors said. Small comfort. She would likely never know the whole story around his illness and death.

Eden closed her eyes and sent up one more prayer. *Lord, help me find my way out of this maze of confusing emotions. Show me the path forward.*

Blake bent over the old motorcycle and checked the oil. It was a congealed mess. The engine wasn't in any better shape. It was frozen solid. He'd have to rebuild it from the bottom up. No surprise since it had been sitting untouched for years. He should have prepared the bike for storage, but he'd left in a hurry. His only thought then was getting away. Now he had a mountain of work to do to get Roxy back in tip-top shape, but reclaiming the old bike would be a joy. This must be the same way Eden felt about Beaumont. Maybe he should have been a little more understanding about her love of the old place. He vowed to make a point to speak more kindly about it in the future.

"I thought I'd find you here. How's Roxy doing?"

Blake wiped his hands on a rag and turned to smile at Jackie. "She'll be good as new with a little work. Nothing too drastic."

Jackie nodded. "Then what? You going to sell her?"

"Bite your tongue, woman. Roxy is family. She's the only memory I want to hang on to from here. I'll never let her go."

Jackie took a step closer. "I heard you toured Beaumont with Eden the other day. She's been working a long time to save that place."

"She certainly has a strong affection for it." Blake stepped to the workbench, gathering his thoughts. "Can I ask you a question about Mark?"

"Sure. I might not know the answer, though."

"Was he a good husband to Eden? A good father to Lucy?" The shadowed look in the woman's eyes sent a twinge of concern through him. He had a feeling he wasn't going to like what he was about to hear.

Jackie took a seat on an old metal stool and crossed her legs. "I wasn't with the family then, but from what I gather, he was a loving husband who adored Eden. Lucy was his pride and joy."

He sensed a *but* coming. "Did he neglect them at all?"

Jackie glanced down at her hands a long moment before answering. "Probably not intentionally. However, Mark was a Sinclair. His first thought was always for the company. From what Eden has told me, there were a lot of missed dinners and events, and trips that got canceled at the last minute. But Eden said she always understood. She loved Mark dearly. She thought he could do no wrong."

"But he did?"

The older woman sighed, then leaned forward. "You have to remember that neither Eden nor Owen knew he was ill. He'd started to complain of headaches, but he always blamed it on the stress of the job. Eden said Mark grew more and more volatile and short-tempered, then he started to withdraw and spent long hours at the Sinclair offices and rarely came home."

"Why didn't Owen do something?"

"I don't think he wanted to face the fact that his son was behaving oddly." She released a breath. "I've tried to talk to Owen, but I think he turned a blind eye to what was happening. To this day he claims things at work were fine and that Mark had kept the company on track."

"And Eden?" Blake asked quietly.

"I think she was lost and confused. She confided in me once that she thought Mark was having an affair and she was crushed."

Blake couldn't imagine his straight-as-an-arrow brother cheating on his wife. Especially someone as amazing as Eden. He cleared his throat to chase away his wayward thought. "That doesn't seem like Mark's style."

"I agree. We were all shocked when we learned he'd been battling cancer."

Blake tried to speak but his voice cracked. "Why didn't he tell anyone? Why suffer alone?"

"I can only guess, but I'd say that he had his father's bullheaded streak and then the tumor changed his personality further, confusing his thinking."

Blake mulled over Jackie's observations the rest of the day. He didn't like what he'd heard, but he had gained a better understanding of Eden and her situation.

What he wanted to know now was, what was his brother going through at the end of his life? Had the tumor been responsible for his drastic change in behavior, or was it something else? A surge of guilt rushed through him. If he'd been here, maybe he could have helped. At least he could try and understand what his brother had endured.

He had an appointment with his new physician tomorrow. Maybe he could get some insight from him.

Something wasn't right about the whole situation, and he wanted answers. And as soon as he could, he would go talk to the man who might have them.

Blake fastened his seat belt a few days later and started the truck. He was still pestered by Eden's comment about Sinclair Properties having difficulties. What had she meant? He'd like to ask his father but that would only create another angry scene.

Turning on his blinker, he headed toward his father's office at the west end of town. Hopefully he'd get answers from his old buddy Norman. They had gone through school together. He, Norman and Tony, Jackie's son, had been inseparable. It would be good to see him again and catch up. A twist of anxiety formed in his chest. He had a feeling that things at the company were more serious than he wanted to believe.

Blake made his way through the entry of Sinclair Properties and up to the second floor, stopping at the first door on the right. It was open and he could see Norman seated at the old walnut desk. His father was overly proud of that desk because his great-great-uncle had commissioned it to be made from timber on the Sinclair property.

Blake tapped lightly on the doorframe. Norman looked up and smiled, motioning him in. His old friend had changed little. He still had the same big smile and red hair. He stood as Blake came near, offering a hand and a pat on the shoulder. "Good to see you, buddy."

Blake held the handshake a moment longer. "It's been a long time." Norman and he had played high school ball together and dated the same girl at one time.

"It's good to see a Sinclair in the building. I'd heard you were back in town. Sit down, fill me in. What brings you back home?" He glanced at the stiff leg and the cane. "And what happened?"

Blake filled him in quickly, skipping the details. "And what about you?"

Norman smiled. "Married Gina Kohl. We have two daughters and a baby boy on the way."

A ping of envy touched Blake's mind. A wife and family. Things he hoped for someday. "That's great to hear."

"What brings you to the office?"

"I'm really here to ask you about the company. Eden hinted that there were problems."

Norman sighed and clasped his hands on the desktop. Blake braced himself for bad news when his friend's expression grew somber. "That's a long story."

"How bad is it?"

"Bad enough that if something isn't done Sinclair Properties might cease to exist. I've tried to get Owen to come back and take the reins, but he won't even consider it."

Blake leaned forward, meeting his old friend's gaze.

"Dad's not himself anymore. He's not happy I'm back, but if the company is in trouble maybe there's something I can do to help."

His friend nodded. "Honestly, I had no idea what kind of chaos I was taking on. I've managed some tough businesses, but Sinclair Properties was the worst I'd seen. It's been two years and I'm still trying to keep the ship from sinking."

"How did it get so bad? Dad was always obsessive about keeping things on track."

Norman dragged his finger over his lower lip. "I don't like to speak ill of the dead, but Mark made a string of poor decisions and over time they led to the cliff we're on right now."

Blake frowned. "That doesn't sound like my brother. What did he do?"

"When I took over, I discovered Mark had purchased a property management company out of Meridian."

"Meridian. Why would he take on something so far away?"

"From what I've learned, Mark was eager to expand the company, only he went about it all wrong. We're a small business with a handful of employees and we weren't equipped on any level to assume the debt of another company. He also made every wrong move possible trying to get things back on track."

"Did you tell Dad about this?"

"Yes. He would nod, then tell me I was doing a good job, and leave. It was like he didn't care what happened to the company at all." Norm took a deep breath. "I managed to unload the Meridian company shortly after I got here, but the damage had already been done. Now it's just a game of dodgeball trying to keep things going."

"What about the properties Dad owns outright? This building and the Grove Hill Mall?"

"Things aren't going well there, either. The mall is old and needs upgrades, but there's no money to do that. The tenants are making noises that they will move to another location if the repairs aren't done." Norman sighed and leaned back in his chair. "If that happens, it's all over."

Blake stood and paced. "This doesn't make sense. Dad was always so fanatical about being responsible to our clients and keeping his properties in order. How could this happen?"

"It only takes one bad decision for things to fall apart. I don't suppose you'd consider coming on board for a while? Our clients might feel more amenable with a Sinclair at the helm."

Blake shook his head. "No. Out of the question. I never wanted to work at this place."

"Then maybe you could talk to your dad, make him see how precarious the situation is. If something doesn't change in the next few months, there won't be a Sinclair Properties. Frankly, I don't know what losing the company would do to his health and I don't want to be responsible for that."

Norman had a point. Sinclair Properties was Owen's driving force. Losing it would be like a knife to his heart—a heart that was fragile. It might literally be the death of him.

"All right. I'll see what I can do."

Blake knew he needed to get to the bottom of this. Fast. Approaching his dad about his company issues would be like lighting a fuse to a box of dynamite, but he had a feeling if he didn't, things would explode.

He stood and held out his hand to his old friend. "Thanks for filling me in. I'll do everything I can to help."

"Don't take too long. I've already started looking for another job."

"Understood. Let me look into things before we talk again."

"I hope you have more success than I did."

Blake left the office with a headache pounding in his skull and a knot in his chest the size of a melon. The decisions his brother had made with the company were mind-boggling. Mark was a levelheaded, conservative man. What had suddenly made him want to take such a risk by expanding the business?

Norman had told him the facts of the situation, but he still wanted to know why. What had been going on with Mark that had upended so many people's lives? Was his tumor to blame or was there something else motivating his decision?

Maybe it was time to look through Mark's files. His family needed answers.

Eden parked her car next to Blake's truck at the museum the next morning and huffed out a sigh. She wasn't looking forward to working with him today. She'd spent a restless night trying to sort out all the conflicting thoughts she'd been having toward her brother-in-law, finally concluding that caution and wisdom should be her guide. Yes, he was different from what she'd expected, and he'd shown her kindness along the way, but he also had a reputation as a charmer. And she would not fall under that spell. She was too smart to get caught in that trap.

Inside the museum, she found the main room empty. Blake wasn't in the office or the kitchen or the storage room. A quick glance out to the yard found no sign of him, either. Where could he be?

"Blake?" Only silence replied.

A faint sound pulled her back into the main room. "Blake?"

"In here."

The reply was so soft she wasn't sure she'd heard it at all. She moved to the door leading to the sanctuary. He was sitting in the second row, staring at the altar. There was a peaceful look on his face she'd never seen before. "Are you okay?"

He grinned and nodded. "I've never been in Saint Joseph's before. This is a peaceful place."

"It's one of the oldest churches in Blessing."

He gestured toward the brass pipes of the old organ that took up the back wall. "Does it work?"

"No. It could but it needs a good bit of restoration."

He fell silent again, and Eden took the opportunity to appreciate the old church. She'd rarely been in the sanctuary since it wasn't slated to be part of the first stage of the museum.

Blake was right. There was an unusual kind of quiet peace here. The shiny pipes of the organ behind the pulpit contrasted with the dark-stained wooden pews waiting silently for the sermon to begin. And the magnificent stained glass windows depicting scenes from the Bible lining both walls shone in the sunlight. Her eyes drifted upward. The hand-carved hanging lights in the ceiling spoke to a slower, more reverent time.

Blake reached for his cane, fingering the handle a moment. "It's a shame it's not a church any longer."

"Saint Joseph's built a new campus. They outgrew this one."

He took one more glance around the room. "My mom would have loved this place. Was Mark a believer?"

It was a question she'd asked herself many times. "He claimed to be."

Blake looked at her, his dark eyes troubled. Her husband's religious beliefs weren't something she wanted to discuss. She squared her shoulders. "There's not much to do today. There's a handful of boxes to go through, and I have labels ready to be placed. Oh, and a bookcase for you to assemble."

"I'm getting pretty good at that." He stood and followed her back to the museum. "By the way, I brought some boxes from the house. Dad said they were important."

Eden frowned. "Okay. We'll go through them later today."

Blake headed to the storage room and she took the opportunity to print out a copy of an old document and slipped it into the small clear case she'd prepared. It was the official record of Blessing becoming the county seat signed by Arthur Avery Sinclair, mayor of Blessing at the time. After carrying the frame to the display cabinet, she stood it up on the middle shelf next to an old photograph of the courthouse during construction under the guidance of engineer William Winslow Sinclair.

She stood back and glanced around. Sometimes she felt as if she were being held captive by Sinclairs. She squelched the unkind thought and went back to work. This was her father-in-law's passion. He had lost so much. It was the least she could do by helping him achieve his dream.

Sounds of hammering filled the air as Blake worked on the bookcase. Eden's heart skipped a beat. *Blake*. She hadn't spoken to him since the tour of Beaumont. He'd taken his meals in the studio, and the few times she'd seen him, he was either playing ball with Lucy or heading toward the car barn, presumably to work on his beloved motorcycle.

At first, she'd been glad he'd stayed away. She needed time to sort through her tangled emotions. The kindness and understanding he'd given her had been difficult to process. She wished he'd been the way she'd expected. It would be easier to deal with him if he was rude and selfish, but he wasn't and that worried her. But she was glad he was here today. She'd started to like him. A lot. Bad idea.

Blake strolled into the display room a few hours later carrying a large box, his cane hooked over his forearm. He set them on a worktable, then coughed as dust flew up around him. She had to smile.

Eden opened the top and peered inside, then blew out a quick breath. "Great, more books and papers. This is going to be more of a library than a museum."

"Maybe we should change the name outside."

She didn't comment. "Every time I think Owen has exhausted his collection of memorabilia, he finds more." Glancing around the main room, she fought off discouragement. She should never have agreed to this job. No matter how much she loved her father-in-law.

Blake looked at her. "I could get started if it would

help. I've got a pretty good idea now what you're looking for."

Eden studied him a moment. That was a mixed blessing. The extra pair of hands and broad shoulders would be more than welcome, but they were attached to a man she needed to avoid. There was an aura about him that made her nervous. Like a stone tossed into a still pond, the ripples just kept expanding.

She forced a smile. "Thanks." On the other hand, many hands make short work. Blake retrieved the second box and placed it on the table. She opened the lid and lifted out an old, faded, moth-eaten uniform jacket. "Ugh."

Blake waved a hand in front of his face. "Is that supposed to be on display?"

"Eventually." She laid the garment aside and reached back into the box, pulling out breeches, a kepi hat and a deteriorated leather shoulder bag.

He winced. "Who do you suppose these belonged to?"

Eden sighed. "Thaddeus Franklin Sinclair. Civil war hero. Died at age nineteen."

"You know way too much about my family history. I've never heard of him." He glanced into the bottom of the cardboard carton and lifted out a wooden box and opened it, emitting a low whistle. The case contained two matching pistols. "These might be worth showing off."

Eden nodded. "At least they're ready to display. The clothing is another matter. What else have we been gifted with?" The third carton contained a small jewelry box resting on top of a set of old dishes and several figurines. She doubted they were worth anything.

Blake had opened up the jewelry box. "Huh. Suppose any of this is real?"

Eden moved to his side and glanced at the sparkling trinkets, lifting one from the box. "It's costume. We might be able to do something with it." She picked up a pocket watch. "I'll research this and see what Owen can tell me. It looks like an old train timepiece. The kind a conductor would carry."

Suddenly tired, she sank down onto the stool. "I thought I was almost done with all the items."

"You can't just lay them on a shelf and call it a day?"

Eden brushed hair from her face. "Yes and no. I can put them in a case quickly, but first I have to label and catalog them so everyone will know what they're looking at."

"How do you do that?"

She gave him a resigned smile. "Sit down with Owen and ask him to tell me about each piece."

Blake groaned. "Glad it's you and not me."

His plaintive attitude made her smile.

Eden closed the box and shoved it aside. The amount of work in those boxes was going to be far more than she could manage. Out of nowhere, a sob rose up in her chest. She pressed her lips together and turned away, hoping Blake hadn't noticed. But he had.

"Hey, you all right?"

He was at her side, scrutinizing her with his dark eyes, stirring up a mixture of emotions in her. It was nice to have someone sensitive to her mood, but she wasn't comfortable with it being Blake. She forced a smile and nodded. "I'm fine. Just tired. I thought we'd been through all the boxes from the attic." She wrapped her arms around her waist. "Sorry."

Blake touched her arm lightly, sending little tingles along her nerves. She told herself to pull away but it felt good to have someone understand and listen.

"Tell me the truth. Is this museum really worth all the trouble?"

"Of course. It'll be a big asset to the town." She hoped her tone was convincing.

He looked skeptical. "Really? A display of all the things the Sinclairs have done over the last two centuries is going to have people lined up to view? It's my family and I wouldn't come to see it."

Eden opened her mouth to protest, then changed her mind. Blake knew the truth. No sense in denying it. "I know it's not a real museum, but I promised Owen I would do this for him and I'm not going to let him down."

"Why are you so loyal to the man? I don't understand."

"Because I love him and I keep my promises." Blake's expression tightened and his jaw flexed. Maybe she should share a little more. "I didn't have a family growing up. Meeting Mark was like a dream come true. He gave me a family, a name and a history, things I never thought I'd have. Owen was kind and welcomed me with open arms."

Blake stood abruptly. "Are you thirsty? How about a glass of tea to chase away that dust."

She nodded. "Thank you." She watched him duck into the kitchen and return with two glasses.

He handed her a glass, his gaze pinning her to the spot. "With all this new stuff, will you be able to have the museum open on time?"

Eden stared at her glass a moment before replying. "I don't know."

"So Dad was right. You do need help."

"Yes, but not just any help. It needs someone in charge who knows what to do. I'm no museum curator. I'm a librarian. Owen thinks that because I work for the Preservation Society I know about museums. I need someone who can do the research and knows the proper way to display things." She blew out a breath. "There are all kinds of requirements for starting a museum."

"Did you try to explain this to him?"

She gave him a smile of resignation. "Several times. He just pats me on the back and tells me how much he believes in me. The way he did Mark."

Blake nodded. "Manipulation technique number one. I've been on the receiving end of that many times."

Her defenses swelled. "He's not trying to be mean… He just wants this so much."

He reached over and laid his hand on hers. "Tell me the truth, Eden. Shouldn't this be in the hands of the local historical society? What do the townspeople think of this?"

Eden bit her lip. She should be supporting her father-in-law, but it felt good to be able to tell the truth to someone. "They aren't happy about it."

"Then why didn't he just donate the building and the items to the city? Shouldn't it be the Blessing History Museum and not the Sinclair Shrine exhibit?"

Eden nodded. "Yes, but Owen wants it private. A public museum was too restrictive and far too complicated. A personal museum has fewer requirements."

Blake made a skeptical grunt. "What he really wants

is total control. The same way he tried to control his sons."

"Try and understand. He lost his dream of Sinclair and Sons. There's no one to leave the company to now. The museum will cement the Sinclair name in the town's memory forever so the contributions of his family over the last hundred and fifty years won't be forgotten."

Blake shook his head. "This is about pride. Nothing else."

"Stop! Don't say that. Can't you understand he's hurting. He's lost his only son and his dream. I won't deny him this small request." She saw Blake stiffen. His expression darkened and his eyes bored into hers.

"His *only* son?"

The sharp edge to his tone sliced through her. Her heart burned, setting every nerve on fire. "Oh, no, I mean… I'm sorry, but you've been gone so long I don't think of you as—" Eden rubbed her temple. She never meant to say anything so cruel to him, but she still couldn't reconcile the Blake that was here with the one she'd heard about for so many years. Her shame gave way to anger, and she faced him. He had no right to be upset. It was all his fault for coming back!

She stood and turned away. "Everything was working fine here until you returned to town. You've upset everything and everyone. Why don't you leave? You're making everything worse."

Blake stood, his eyes dark and stormy, his jaw rigid. Pivoting on his heel, he turned and walked out, shutting the door quietly behind him.

Eden put her hands on her face and cried. How could

she have been so unfeeling? She'd hurt Blake to the core because she hadn't been thinking.

And because her feelings toward him were growing murky.

Chapter Eight

Blake drove home struggling to decide if he was hurt or just angry. Eden's comment had pierced his spirit like a scalding-hot sword. He was still bleeding from the words. He was also furious at Owen for taking advantage of Eden, and at Eden for being so blindly loyal to his father. And deep down he resented being shoved back into the bad-boy role again. But Eden was right in one regard. He had been gone a long time. She had never met him so all she had to go on were the things Mark and his dad had told her, which apparently were all damning.

He parked the car and sought refuge in the studio. His leg was throbbing. He'd carried those boxes and now he was paying the price. Swallowing two pills, he eased onto the sofa, his heart still stinging. *"His only son."* He'd hoped Eden's opinion of him had softened. He wanted to be her friend. Family. He'd felt a bond starting between him and his sister-in-law. He thought they were reaching common ground, and a comfortable working relationship. But it had all been shattered with three words.

While he admired Eden's loyalty to his dad, he felt it was misplaced. Owen was a master manipulator, skilled at getting his own way. Blake just didn't want her to be taken advantage of. She was too honest and kind. She was everything a man could want. Everything he admired in a woman.

He rested his head on the back of the sofa. Time to be honest. He was strongly attracted to his sister-in-law. Eden was starting to seep into his system. Bad idea. He'd caused enough animosity in his family. Having feelings for his brother's wife would be the ultimate sin.

Blake rubbed his eyes. But the more he was around her, the more he was drawn. He had to get his mind off Eden. He caught sight of Mark's computer. He hadn't looked at it since he talked to Norman. Maybe now would be a good time. He needed to figure out why his brother made such a mistake and he needed a distraction from thinking about Eden.

Did she really want him to leave or was she upset by his comments about Owen? Maybe they both needed time apart. He certainly did. His attraction to Eden was growing stronger every day. He'd even started dreaming about her. She'd flitted in and out of his dreams, flashing a smile or a wave. He'd see her walking across the lawn with Lucy, the sunlight kissing her hair. He'd tried to ignore his feelings, but it was getting harder each day.

Somehow, he had to find a way to shut down his infatuation before it got out of hand.

If he didn't, he could say goodbye to any connection to his family forever.

* * *

Eden went in search of Jackie and found her curled up with a book in the living room. She glanced up and smiled. As Eden approached, her smile faded.

"Oh dear. I know that look. What's on your mind, Edie?" She patted the cushion beside her. "Come sit down."

Eden eased down, welcoming the touch of Jackie's hand on her knee. "I did something horrible today and I don't know what to do about it."

"I doubt you could do anything horrible, but go ahead. What was it?"

"Blake and I were at the museum talking and he said some things about Owen that upset me, and I tried to explain why the museum is so important to him and me." She covered her mouth with one hand. "I told him that Owen was still hurting for losing his only son."

Jackie inhaled a slow breath. "I see. Well, that sure comes close to being horrible."

Eden's eyes teared up. "It is, isn't it? I don't know what I was thinking. I tried to explain but then I got mad and told him he was ruining everything here and he should just leave."

"What did Blake do?"

"He just turned to stone and he didn't say a word." She wiped at her tears. "He just walked out. I don't know how to fix this."

"An apology would be a good start."

She nodded. "I know and I will but I'm so ashamed I don't think I can face him. I never meant to hurt him like that."

"Which bothers you more, that you hurt him or that you asked him to leave?"

Eden slumped back on the sofa. "Both."

"Do you think he's ruining everything? More importantly, do you really want him to leave?"

The questions brought her up short. Did she? "No. But everything is changing since he returned. Owen is hateful to him, and I don't understand why. Lucy loves him and I don't understand that, either. It's like he's uncovering all these hidden parts of the family."

"Maybe it was time," Jackie murmured.

Eden released a quavering breath. "He's not like I expected."

"In what way?"

"*Every* way. He's calm, steady. He was a policeman, not a daredevil, and he's kind and patient and understanding and thoughtful." She sat up and clasped her hands in her lap. "He's easy to talk to. He understands where I'm coming from. With Mark, sometimes it was as if we spoke two different languages."

"And you're developing feelings for him."

"No, of course not! I mean I like him, but he's Mark's brother."

"What does that have to do with anything?"

Eden recoiled inwardly, horrified at the suggestion. "Jackie, that would be wrong. Shameful. It would be like betraying my husband."

"Why? He's not here any longer."

"I couldn't stand the guilt," Eden admitted.

"Guilt over what? Loving again?"

"Yes, I'm not ready."

"Widows remarry all the time. We're allowed to fall in love, to live again. Would you be surprised to know that I'm falling in love again and I've been a widow for eight years?" Jackie sighed softly. "Yes, I feel bad sometimes and worry what my husband would think. Especially since the man is so very different from William."

"Really? Who is it?"

Jackie waved off the question. "Not important. Would it help you to know that Blake is falling in love with you?"

Eden had never considered such a thing. "No. You're wrong."

"I see the signs. I've known him longer than you. I knew him before he went away, and I know how much he's changed. The man that returned home is not the same one who walked out all those years ago."

Eden stood and paced. "I don't know what to do. Everything is so messed up."

"Perhaps you need someone wiser than me to discuss this with?"

She realized exactly what Jackie was suggesting and she was ashamed she hadn't thought of it herself. Time to visit the Blessing Bridge again.

But what if she didn't find her answers there, either?

Eden toyed with the glass in her hand and stared out the sitting room window at the winter gloom hovering over the area today. She should be getting ready for work but she lacked the motivation. Winter in Mississippi was always a roller-coaster ride. She was glad the winters were short, barely two months. But just when you got used to the temperate days, the chill factor would return and plunge everything into the cold. It made for a constant change of wardrobe from day to day.

"Eden." Jackie walked toward her. "I forgot to tell

you Owen's doctor's appointment was changed, and we have to be there at four this afternoon. So you'll have to take Lucy to dance class."

"All right. I'm sure I can get away a little early."

The older woman placed a hand on her shoulder. "You feeling any better about Blake?"

She nodded. "I still have to apologize. I'm just waiting for the right moment."

"Uh-huh. Take it from me, right moments rarely materialize. Just walk up to him and say you're sorry."

Eden wished it was that simple. Her visit to the bridge the other day hadn't been easy, but it had given her the courage and conviction to tell Blake how sorry she was and that she didn't really want him to leave. That had been a hard realization. She liked her brother-in-law. A lot. *Too much.* He was taking up space in her thoughts more and more.

Her cell phone rang, drawing her from her confused thoughts. Her boss was calling. Probably wondering why she was late for work. She should have been at the office twenty minutes ago. "Hi, Virginia. I'll be there soon."

"I have good news. The heirs to Beaumont have reached a consensus. They want to sell the house to us. All we need to do is agree on a price."

Eden yelped. "Really? That's wonderful! I can't believe it. I'd given up hope."

"Me, too. We have a conference call here today at four o'clock to discuss it. Don't be late."

"I won't." She ended the call and spun around with happiness. She had to tell Blake.

Grabbing a sweater, she hurried to the studio and knocked. No answer. His vehicle was parked in the drive so that meant he was working on Roxy. She hurried across the lawn and through the door of the car barn and to the back corner. He was there, bent over the motorcycle. She was always intrigued by the joy he found in the old machine.

She was suddenly tense. They hadn't spoken since her hurtful comment. He looked up and saw her.

"Hey." He smiled and her heart skipped a beat. It shouldn't. Apparently, Blake didn't hold a grudge. "How's Roxy?"

"Coming along. You look happy. Did you get good news?"

She could barely contain her excitement. "My boss just called. We might get Beaumont after all."

He set aside the tool he'd been holding. "That's great news. You must be overjoyed."

"I am." A part of her wished there wasn't a bike between them because she would like to have given Blake a hug. "We have a videoconference this afternoon to go over things." She stopped. "Oh, I forgot. Lucy has dance class this afternoon and Jackie is taking Owen to an appointment."

"I could take her."

She blinked. Had he just offered to take a five-year-old to a dance class? "Oh no. I couldn't ask you to do that. I'll call one of the other mothers and see if they can pick her up."

"I don't mind. Really."

His kindness reminded her of something she'd been putting off. "Blake. I want to apologize for what I said at the museum the other day. It was thoughtless and cruel, and I didn't think. I never meant to say something so unkind. Please, can you forgive me?"

"I already have. You know, it was never my intention to disrupt things here. I underestimated my father's capacity for holding a grudge. I never wanted to make everyone miserable."

"You haven't, and I don't want you to leave. Lucy would miss you." Heat shot up into her neck. She'd almost said she'd miss him, too. Big mistake.

"I'd miss her, too. Well, I'd better get cleaned up. I have a date with a sweet little lady."

Blake stepped into the kitchen of the main house later that day and was grabbed at the knees by a ponytailed princess. He chuckled. He'd never felt such a warm, happy sensation. This must be what being a dad felt like. He bent and patted Lucy's back. "I'm happy to see you, too."

"I'm glad you're taking me to dance. You can see my purple tutu. It's gonna be so much fun!"

He wasn't sure about that, but he smiled. How could he not with those big blue eyes looking up at him. "Awesome."

Eden came toward him from the sitting room. "I can't thank you enough for this. I hope you don't regret it."

Blake laid a hand on Lucy's shoulder. "No way. I love being with my niece. All I need is directions."

Eden smirked. "You might need more than that. You do realize you'll be surrounded by little girls, laughing and screaming the whole hour." She leaned toward him and lowered her voice. "Just FYI, little girls scream over everything." She shrugged as if to say there was nothing he could do about it. "But you'll have the other mothers to help you out."

Lucy looked up at him with sparkling eyes. "You can meet my friend Addie. She's my bestest friend ever."

Blake glanced at Eden. "Everyone should have a best friend." Were he and Eden becoming friends? He hoped so. He looked at the little girl, who had taken his hand in hers. "Are you ready to go?" She nodded. "Are you driving?" Lucy giggled and his heart did that warm melty thing again.

"No, silly. I'm too little."

"Then I guess it's up to me."

Eden ran her hand over her daughter's blond hair and smiled at him. "You'll have to take my car. It has the child seat."

They exchanged keys. "Where are we going?"

"Tina Corday's School of Dance. Duncan Street just off the square."

A jolt of alarm shot through him. What did he know about tutus, or five-year-old little girls for that matter? He looked at Eden, who gave him an encouraging pat on the shoulder.

"Don't worry. All you have to do is watch."

Feeling somewhat relieved, he smiled at Lucy. "Then let's head out."

He found the studio with no trouble, but when they got inside, he had no idea where to go. His niece tugged him along to the dressing room now filled with a half dozen little girls in various stages of costumes.

Blake felt like a bull in a china shop. His six-foot-two frame wasn't designed to fit in this little room. Lucy sat on the floor and unzipped her small satchel. She pulled out a length of purple nylon and held it up to him. "I need help with my tights."

Blake looked at the stretchy purple fabric. It had a

waistband, but he had no earthly idea how to get the thing on the little girl.

A hand lightly touched his shoulder. "I can do that."

He looked up at a slender woman with kind eyes. "Thanks. I'm out of my comfort zone here."

She started to gather up one leg of the garment, then proceeded to slip it over Lucy's foot before quickly repeating the process. Once the child was on her feet, the purple nylon fit her little legs perfectly. Next came a purple body suit with a ring of fluff around Lucy's hips. Suddenly she looked like a miniature ballerina and Blake's heart melted like warm butter.

Lucy hurried out with the other girls and the woman introduced herself. "I'm Shirley Kirby, a close friend of Eden's. You must be Blake Sinclair."

"Guilty."

"Let's go find a seat."

Blake was intrigued by the little girls fluttering around the large dance floor.

"I've heard a lot about you."

Blake grimaced. "Ouch. I'm afraid I'm not Eden's favorite person." Though he hoped that was changing. Maybe his trip to dance class would earn him some brownie points.

"I wouldn't be too sure of that. She told me how you helped her at Beaumont the other day and what a help you've been at the museum."

"I'm glad I was able to help. She's a very…" He chose his words carefully. "Capable woman."

Virginia gave him a skeptical glance. "Um. She's more than that. But I'm sure you've discovered her other sterling qualities."

Blake was grateful when the teacher called the class

to attention. He was well aware of Eden's many attractive assets, but he wasn't about to voice them to anyone right now.

Dance class had started, and Blake kept his gaze trained on his niece. She wasn't the best dancer in the group, but what she lacked in coordination she made up for with enthusiasm. He found himself chuckling at her happy movements. She smiled at him and waved, and his heart started the quick melt again.

For the first time in years, he allowed himself to think about a family of his own.

When the instructor dismissed the class, Lucy raced toward him all smiles. "Did you see me dance?"

"I did. You were the best one of all."

She giggled and gave him a hug. Blake looked at her precious face and realized he wasn't ready for their time to end. "I think we need to celebrate. How about we go for ice cream?"

"Yay! I'll hurry and change."

Blake looked at her tiny purple ballerina outfit. "I think you should leave it on. Then everyone will know you're a dancer."

She thought about that a second, then nodded.

The ice-cream shop was still in the same spot he remembered. After selecting their flavors, they sat by the window to eat.

A woman walked by and stopped. "Oh, how adorable. You are the cutest ballerina I've ever seen."

Lucy smiled. "Thank you."

"And so polite. You and your wife have done a good job with this little one."

Blake returned the lady's smile but his throat was so tight he couldn't speak. Lucy, his child. What a bless-

ing that would be. He'd be proud to call her his own.
He'd be proud to claim Eden as his also.

He shook off the notion. That would never, ever
happen.

But it was nice to think about.

Eden heard Blake breaking down boxes in the storage room Saturday morning and sighed in relief. After
her cruel comment last week about Mark being the
only son, she feared he wouldn't come to work today.
Though he'd been more than willing to take Lucy to
dance class. Her daughter was still talking about how
much fun they'd had and begging for him to take her
again next week.

After placing her belongings in the office, she went
in search of her helper, hoping her father-in-law had
exhausted his collection and hadn't sent more boxes.
She found Blake in the kitchen holding a cup of coffee.
The sense of relief that he was here washed through
her with more force than she expected. "Good morning." The smile he gave her sent a warm tingle down
her spine. There should be laws against a smile like
that. "Did you bring any more boxes?"

He chuckled. "Nope. I guess that means we're all
out of important Sinclair memorabilia."

"Let's hope so."

It was late morning when Eden took a moment to
step back and examine their work. They'd made good
progress. Blake had assembled the last few shelves and
cabinets, and she'd made as many information labels
as she could. Though some were simply described as
old watch, or *antique jewelry*. Owen had been reluctant
to share his stories with the last boxes he'd donated.

Strange since he was always up to bragging about his family and their treasures.

Eden tapped her lower lip with her thumb. She'd been discouraged this morning when she came to the museum. Blake was right. No one would come to see this collection of Sinclair belongings. They were a part of Blessing history but not the whole history.

Blake stepped into the room, brushing dust from his shirt. As much as she'd resented him helping, he'd proved to be a blessing. And she'd come to enjoy his company.

"I'm starved. How about I run and get us something from the deli?"

It sounded good and her stomach was rumbling. "Okay." She gave him her order. He smiled, then gave her a little salute and left. She noticed he wasn't using his cane today. He must be feeling stronger. She'd worried the other day when she'd noticed him leaning on it heavily.

Walking to the side window, she looked out to the grassy side yard of the old church. There, under the sprawling branches of a giant magnolia tree, was a picnic table. After inhaling all that stale dusty air from the boxes, fresh air sounded like a wonderful idea. Eden gathered up utensils and paper plates and carried them out to the picnic table. She added a red, yellow and green plaid tablecloth for a splash of color to the drab landscape. As a final touch, she picked a few camellia blooms and placed them in a paper cup on the table.

She loved decorating and preparing a meal for her family. It was something she and Mark rarely did because he was always tied up at work. Quickly, she shoved that negative memory aside.

"Eden?"

"Out here." Blake emerged from the side door and winked as he approached the picnic table. "This is a great idea. I haven't been on a picnic in years."

"I thought we needed a little fresh air after all that dust."

"Agreed." He stepped over the seat and sat down. "It's a perfect day, too. Temperatures in the seventies, a clear sky overhead and a gentle breeze." He leaned forward and grinned. "The forecast calls for this to continue through Mardi Gras next week."

"That would be nice. It's been too cold the last few years to enjoy the parades." Eden handed him a paper plate and fished out the sandwiches from the bag.

Blake took a bite of his sandwich. "Did we accomplish much this morning?"

Eden took a moment to reply. "We did. I'm afraid there's not much more that can be done. The bicentennial is only five weeks away and there's no way I can get this place the way Owen wants it in time."

"I'm sure he'll understand. Though I still think a soup kitchen or homeless shelter would have been a better idea."

"Certainly easier. I wouldn't have to face your father at the end of the day and report that I didn't get much done."

"Yeah, that has to be tough," Blake murmured. "Did you and Mark always live at Oakley Hall?"

She toyed with her drink container for a long moment. "No. We had a home in Bridge Way Estates. Lucy and I moved here after Mark died." Might as well tell him the whole story. "I had to sell the house after he passed away. Owen offered to let us live with him."

His eyes widened. "You had to sell your home?"

She nodded and folded the edge of her napkin back and forth. "The house, the contents, the cars, the boat. All of it. Mark developed a gambling habit and he lost everything we had. He left me with a mountain of debt to pay. I'm grateful for Owen taking us in."

Blake set his jaw. "I can't believe my brother would be so careless. And *gambling*? That doesn't make sense. You must have been furious."

She studied her hand. How could she ever explain the pendulum of emotions during that time? "I was in shock. I was horrified, hurt and angry. Mark died in a car accident, so there was an autopsy. That's when we learned about the tumor. How could I blame him for something that wasn't his fault?"

"That's very generous of you. But I don't think I could be so forgiving. Especially after learning he kept his illness to himself."

"I wasn't. I still have moments when I'm so angry that I... But I had Lucy to think of. Being angry all the time wouldn't be good for her."

"No, of course not."

A squirrel hopped onto the end of the table, chirped and rose on its hind legs. "Oh, look. Isn't he cute?"

"And hungry." Blake tossed a piece of his roll out onto the ground. The squirrel glanced at each of them as if saying thank you, then hopped down, grabbed the treat and scampered off under the tree. "That's the closest I've been to a squirrel."

Blake was staring at her. His dark eyes held a light of affection she'd never seen before. Was Jackie right...? Was he attracted to her? Did she want him to be? What if he was? What then?

She searched for a more comfortable topic of conversation, but Owen marched out into the yard.

"What are you doing playing outside when there is work to do?"

Blake met her gaze, his jaw flexing. "We're eating lunch, Dad."

Eden spoke up. "It was such a nice day and I thought we needed a break."

"I saw the boxes inside strewn all over the place. Why aren't the items I sent over on display?"

"They will be, but I have to catalog them first, then—"

Owen waved off her explanation. "Nonsense. Hang it up, put a sign on it and move on. Time is short."

Owen pinned Blake with a cold stare. "This is all your fault. Always looking for a way to shirk your responsibilities. Get it together. This is important."

Eden opened her mouth to respond but the man pivoted on his heel and walked away.

Blake exhaled an angry breath. "I'm sorry. He has no right to talk to you like that. He's always been oblivious to others' feelings."

Eden folded her napkin. Blake was proving to be right. "I don't think the museum will ever satisfy Owen, no matter how hard I work."

"No, it won't. He's asking the impossible."

"I don't like to fail. I keep my promises."

"Some promises can't be kept. No matter how much we'd like them to."

Eden nodded. "You're right but how do you keep from feeling like a failure?"

Blake reached over and squeezed her hand. "You

could never be a failure at anything you put your heart into."

His encouraging words lingered in her heart for a long time.

Chapter Nine

Blake closed his brother's journal and leaned back in the recliner. Reading Mark's private thoughts was awkward and disheartening. He battled guilt each time he opened the cover. But he was also beginning to understand what was going on in Mark's mind and the pressure he'd been under.

He rubbed the cover with his thumb. His older sibling had kept his cancer and the problems at work from Eden because he didn't want to upset her. Unfortunately, the progression of his tumor had started to distort his thought process. The last entry Blake had read revealed Mark's sense of panic that he might lose the company. His fear of letting Owen down had brought Blake near tears. He delved into how much their dad trusted him to take the company from a small firm to something bigger. And how terrified he was of never bringing that dream to fruition.

But the comment that had torn Blake's heart to shreds was when Mark wrote that Owen had told him to grow the business or resign. He knew that feeling of receiving an ultimatum from their father, but he never expected it to be directed to Mark.

Blake stood and went to the window. It was clear that Owen had been pushing Mark to expand the company, and his brother never considered standing up to their father.

The question now was, what did he do with this information? If he told Eden, it might destroy her memories of her husband. And if he confronted his dad over what he'd learned, it might kill him. How would he handle the truth? Was it worth the risk that it could bring on another attack? But did he have a right to keep this discovery to himself?

He shoved a hand through his hair, his mind whirling. And then there was the matter of Sinclair Properties. If it was going to survive, then things had to change. His dad had to come out of his fog of denial and step up.

As far as he could see, there was only one way to tackle this, and that was head-on. He had to talk to his father. If the company was going to be saved, something had to change. There was no one else who had a chance of getting through to Owen. It was up to him.

And, as it turned out, there was no time like the present. Eden was at work, Lucy was at school and Jackie was running errands. Inhaling a fortifying breath, he made his way to the main house. Owen was in the living room reading. Blake watched him a moment. For the first time since coming home, he took a good look at his father and realized with a jolt how old he looked. He was in his midsixties, but he looked older, as if life had worn him down. A heart attack and the aftermath could explain it but maybe it was something more.

"Dad. We need to talk."

Owen didn't budge. "No. We don't."

"We do if you want Sinclair Properties to survive."

Owen looked up, his eyes narrowed. "I'm not discussing my company with you."

Blake took a seat on the coffee table, close enough to his father to see his eyes. "You'd better or it'll be gone forever." Owen grunted and looked at his book. "I've talked to Norman, Dad. He told me about the trouble the company is facing."

"He had no right to tell you anything."

He leaned forward. "The company is failing, and he puts the blame on you and Mark. I want to know what happened."

"Not your concern. Norman is in charge, and he'll work it out."

Blake kept a tight rein on his temper. "Why are you turning a blind eye to this? Sinclair Properties has been your passion for as long as I can remember. Why did you step away from it?"

"Mark has everything under control," Owen bit out.

Blake reared back. "Mark is gone, Dad. Norman is in charge."

The look on his father's face sent a chill down Blake's spine. Shock. Fear. Horror. All emotions he'd never seen his father display.

"I said *Norman*. Don't put words in my mouth."

Blake set his jaw. Time to pull off the Band-Aid. "Why did Mark buy that Meridian company? We're a small business. We couldn't afford to take on another business."

Owen's eyes widened. "I wouldn't know. Maybe he wanted to grow the company." Owen stood and walked to the fireplace, keeping his back to his son.

Blake's heart sank. His suspicions were verified. "Did you push him to expand? Is that why he rushed into the deal?"

"Mark was his own man. I didn't question his decisions."

He chewed his lip. "Maybe you should have. That one mistake put the company in jeopardy. It may not recover if someone doesn't take charge. It's time to go back to work, Dad. If you don't you could lose it all."

"Mark knew what he was doing."

"No, he didn't. He was sick and he wasn't thinking clearly. The more he tried to fix things, the worse they got. Why didn't you stop him? Why didn't you take matters into your own hands?" Owen remained silent and closed off. "Dad, you have to open your eyes. Norman says you'll have to file bankruptcy soon if something doesn't change."

"That's not true. It'll be fine. Once the museum is done…"

Blake could maintain his composure no longer. "Stop it! Stop thinking about that museum and focus on the business. And stop expecting Eden to fulfill your dream. It's unfair." He jumped to his feet and glared down at his father. "She'd do anything for you and you're taking advantage of her. She has enough on her plate with a job and Lucy. She doesn't need your pet project on top of that. She's working overtime, worried she'll let you down, and for what? A place no one will come to see."

Jackie hurried into the room. "What's all the shouting about? Owen, you need to calm down. Take a few deep breaths." The man waved off her concern with a growl. "Blake, what's going on?"

Blake crossed his arms over his chest. "I just found out that the company is falling apart because of something Mark did, but Dad won't do anything about it."

Jackie took his arm and steered him to the kitchen. "Sit down. I'll be right back."

Blake leaned back in the chair and tried to calm himself. What was wrong with his dad that he wouldn't fight for his business? It was alarming.

Jackie returned and took a seat at the table. "He's calmed down for the moment. Now tell me what's going on."

"What's going on is that he acts like he doesn't care if the company folds or not. Worse, he talked as if Mark was still here."

She sighed and nodded. "He's in denial. Has been since shortly after Mark passed. When we learned about the tumor, it upset everyone. Eden had been furious about losing her home and being left broke. But she changed when she learned Mark had been ill."

"And Dad?"

Jackie shook her head. "He grieved hard. He tried to go back to the office but after a few months he came home and shut down. I had a feeling something happened, but I never found out what. I think he's trapped in his grief. He's channeled it into that museum." She leaned toward him. "For some reason he can't fully accept that Mark is gone."

"Does he know about the mistakes Mark made at work? The mess he created?"

"I don't know. He doesn't talk about the company anymore."

"Something has to happen to wake him up. He needs to know what Mark did."

"It might be too much for him to handle."

A wash of concern replaced Blake's irritation. "Is his heart condition that precarious?"

"It's bad, but no, Owen likes to play it up for the attention."

"Yeah. No surprise there. Still, his whole life was in the company. What changed?"

Jackie shrugged. "Mark died and his big dream along with him. I can't get through to him."

"Well, someone better or Sinclair Properties will be gone."

Jackie held his gaze. "I'm not sure he would care."

Blake was still simmering with frustration over his father's lack of concern for the business well into the evening. He'd eaten alone, unwilling to face Owen again. From his front window, he'd watched the family around the table. They weren't smiling or even talking, from what he could tell. Even when he wasn't in the house, he had the ability to upset everyone.

He rubbed his jaw. Maybe Eden was right. Coming home had only stirred up a hornet's nest of problems and old resentments. Feeling restless and trapped, he went out onto the porch and sat in the rocker. The cold evening air calmed his tension and chased the fog from his brain.

He closed his eyes and concentrated on the soothing motion of the old chair.

"Blake!"

He opened his eyes and saw Eden running toward him, putting his heart rate into overdrive. Something was wrong. He hurried to greet her. "What's happened?"

"Beaumont is on fire!"

"What?" He took her shoulders in his hands. She was shaking and the pain in her blue eyes tore at his heart.

She clutched at his arm. "Virginia just called. It's on fire. I've got to go. Will you take me?"

His first inclination was to agree, but then his practical mind kicked in. "I'm not sure that's a good idea. You won't be able to get close. The fire department will be there, and the police will have it blocked off."

"I know but I have to be there." She grabbed his shirtfront. "Please, Blake."

He nodded. He would take her, but he'd make sure she stayed far away from the chaos. "Come on."

He kept one hand in hers as he drove, second-guessing his choice. He should have convinced her to stay at home where she'd be safe, but he knew how much the old house meant to her, and how hard she'd worked to save it.

Eden didn't speak on the ride. She held his hand and stared out the window, crying silent tears that clawed at his heart.

The driveway to Beaumont was blocked off, but other gawkers were standing up on the lawn. Eden was out of the car before he could stop her. "Eden, wait!"

She pushed through the spectators, only stopping when the policeman stepped in front of her. Blake stood behind her, taking her shoulders in his hands. She was shaking, tears were streaming down her cheeks and she muttered softly.

The roof of the rear addition collapsed with a loud noise and sparks shot into the sky. One wall broke loose, sending bricks tumbling to the ground with sickening thuds and stirring up ashes as they hit the ground.

"Oh no."

Eden's soft cry raked over his nerves. "Maybe we should go." Watching this had to be torture for her.

She shook her head. "No. I have to be here."

Firefighters turned their hoses on the central portion, keeping the roof wet in an attempt to save it.

They watched as the flames relentlessly consumed the original wooden structure and advanced to the Greek Revival addition at the front. Eden shuddered each time a portion fell prey to the flames. He wished he could do something to help, but all he could do was stand with her and offer what little comfort there was.

The firemen were working to contain the fire but even she could see it was hopeless. A house this old would succumb quickly to the blaze. She yelped when the west side of the home collapsed, crumbling into a pile on the ground, leaving only the chimney chase standing.

She turned her face into his shoulder. And he cradled her head with his hand. A loud popping pulled her attention back around. The fire had leaped onto the roof of the Greek Revival home in the front and was devouring it like tissue paper. Even the firefighters had turned their attention to keeping the flames contained.

There was no hope of saving the historic home. A piece of Blessing was now a pile of smoldering ashes.

As they watched, the upper gallery, where he'd stood a short while ago, tilted, then tumbled to the ground amid plumes of ash and debris. The lower gallery was quickly devoured. The death throes of the old house were the hiss and pop of the remnants of its life slowly ceasing.

Eden had turned and buried her face against his chest. Her trembling had eased but he could sense she was drained and weak. "Are you all right?"

She nodded. With nothing more to see, Blake gently turned her away, keeping his arm around her shoulders. She walked with unsteady steps as they made their way to the car. The smell of smoke hung in the air, leaving an acrid taste in their mouths. He could only imagine the emotional pain Eden must be in. He needed to get her someplace quiet and safe.

He reached to open the car door when she looked up at him, her eyes brimming with tears.

"It's gone, Blake. It's all gone." A sob caught in her throat.

He pulled her into his arms and made soothing noises. He felt so helpless.

She looked up at him again and his heart rate tripled. She was so beautiful, such a strong, kind, amazing woman, and he was falling in love with her.

She said his name, softly, holding his gaze. The air around them stilled, grew warm, and he was aware of her breath, the little pulse in her neck. He tilted his head, drawn toward her with a power he didn't understand.

Mark.

She was his brother's wife. He braced and stepped

away. Eden blinked, held his gaze a moment longer, then turned and got into the car.

Blake limped to the driver's side, his emotions surging like a tsunami. He fumbled with the keys, fighting to regain control of himself. They rode in silence toward home. Eden's sorrow was like a third person in the vehicle. "How are you doing?"

She wiped tears from her cheeks. "I'm fine."

"I'm sorry. I know how much that place meant to you."

She nodded. "We've been working so hard to save it and the heirs were finally coming together. Now, it's gone."

Blake glanced at her. "I wonder what started the fire."

She shrugged. "It could have been anything. A house this old can have any number of threats. It doesn't matter. That part of our town history is lost."

Blake heard the agony in her voice and longed to comfort her somehow. He searched for an appropriate way.

"Would you like to stop for a drink to gather yourself? The coffee shop should still be open." He braced for her to refuse. He was sure she wanted to go home and grieve for a while.

"I'd like that. Thank you."

Seated near the window of the small café, Eden savored the richness of the special roast brew. There were few people in the café, but those who were there were all abuzz about the fire. The house had been important to all of Blessing. Its loss would be keenly felt, especially during this bicentennial year.

She turned her gaze to the window, enjoying the lights of the downtown. Blessing had donned a sparkling facade this year in celebration of its anniversary.

Her nerves calmed and her emotions began to settle into place. She found Blake's quiet demeanor comforting. He'd brought her coffee to the table and sat silently, not attempting any conversation. She was grateful. Mark always felt he had to be talking, solving a problem. He'd never understood that sometimes she just needed to soak up the silence.

Blake was a more comfortable companion. He'd been so kind to bring her to the old house despite his objections, and he'd stood by protectively as the house was destroyed. It was something Mark wouldn't have even thought of doing. He never understood her love of old homes.

The thought shocked her, and she took a quick sip of her brew to regain her composure. And to avoid looking at her brother-in-law. She had to stop comparing the brothers. Not only was it pointless but it was an affront to Mark. Yet, she found herself doing it more than she should.

To her dismay, each day she saw a different side of Blake. She'd seen his gentle way with Lucy and Cuddles, his patience with Owen and his dedication to helping at the museum. Now his tender compassion and consideration were starting to endear him to her even more.

"If you're done with your coffee, I thought you might like to take a walk along the river."

The sound of his voice jolted her back to reality. Being outside sounded like a good idea. They were too close here in the small coffee shop.

They walked in silence down the block and onto the sloping sidewalk that curled along the edge of the river. The city had turned the once-overgrown bank into a charming garden of lights and flowers and cozy seating.

"I love it down here. I wish I could come here more often."

"It's quite a change from what I remember."

As they walked, her grief began to surface again, her mind filled with the horrific image of flames and the house crumbling into the ground. "I loved that house. It was special."

"But it meant something more to you."

"Yes. I felt an attachment to it from the moment I came to Blessing," she admitted. "Then when I went to work with the preservation group and learned about its history and the families that lived there, I wanted to save it. I think in the back of my mind I adopted it. Silly, huh? But it felt like home. I even mentioned to Mark that one day we might be able to buy it."

"Did he like the idea?" he asked.

"No. He had a different kind of home in mind. We built it the next spring."

Blake reached over and squeezed her hand, and she squeezed back, unwilling to break the contact. She stole a quick glance at him. He'd almost kissed her back at the house. She wouldn't have resisted if he had. But she'd seen the light dawn in his eyes, the realization that she was his brother's wife. She appreciated his strength of character. He was far stronger than her.

The problem was, now she would be tormented by the thought of what his kiss would have been like. Her cheeks flamed. She slipped her hand from his. "I think I need to go home now."

Blake gave her an encouraging smile and they turned their steps back toward the car.

Eden watched with a smile as Lucy and Cuddles played on the rug in the kitchen sitting room. The picture warmed her heart. It was moments like this that helped her keep the loss of Beaumont in perspective. She grieved the demise of the old home, but she was so blessed in her personal life she had little cause to be sad for long. Blake's sincere compassion had helped, too.

"Mommy, I want Uncle Blake to come to my daddy-daughter lunch tomorrow."

Her contented mood vanished. "Wouldn't it be nicer if Grandpa came instead?"

"No. Uncle Blake looks more like a daddy."

She had a point, but the idea didn't sit well. "I'm not sure Uncle Blake could come. He might be busy tomorrow."

"No, he's not. I already asked him."

Wonderful. How did she navigate this one? Blake enjoyed time with Lucy, she had no doubt about that. But standing in for his brother, taking the role of father, might be asking too much. "We'll see. I'll talk to Uncle Blake, okay?"

Eden was still mulling over how to broach the topic of stand-in dad when Blake entered the kitchen a short while later. "I ran across a box of my grandfather's belongings in the car barn. You might want to take a look and see if they would add to the museum displays."

"Oh goody. More stuff." She smirked. "We can always use more Sinclair artifacts." She heard Blake chuckle. "Sorry."

He waved off her concern. "Hey, I'm on your side, remember?"

She did and she was more grateful than she should be. "While you're here, I understand Lucy asked you to go to the school lunch tomorrow."

He smiled. "You mean the daddy-daughter thing. Yeah, I was flattered. But I didn't commit. I wasn't sure how you felt about it."

How *did* she feel? On one hand, she wanted her daughter to have a parent with her for the special event, but having Blake take the place of her father left her feeling guilty. "I suppose it would be all right. But don't feel obligated."

"Are you kidding? I'm looking forward to it. We're buddies. And I kinda like the idea of being a parent. I hope to try it myself someday."

The thought popped into her mind that he would be a wonderful father. She squelched that thought and opened her laptop and got to work.

Eden rubbed her eyes an hour later and looked up and smiled. Lucy was draped over the back of the easy chair by the sitting room window, staring outside. Cuddles was up on his hind legs beside her. She was glad her daughter was so close to her uncle. He was a noble role model.

Owen strolled into the kitchen and stopped beside Lucy looking out the window.

"What are you staring at?"

Lucy smiled at her grandpa. "That place." She pointed to the car barn.

"Why?"

Eden smiled at the gruff tone in Owen's voice.

"I'm waiting for Uncle Blake to come out so he can play with me."

Her father-in-law turned to her for an explanation. Eden stood and came to his side. "They play soccer every day."

"There he is." Lucy scrabbled out of the chair and dashed to the back door, Cuddles on her heels.

Eden watched with Owen as the pair nearly knocked Blake over with their excitement. He lifted Lucy with one arm and swung her around, then bent down to tussle with the dog. She noticed he was using his cane today. Was he hurting? He had a habit of not acknowledging when he was in pain. Like father like son. But at least Blake knew enough to use the cane when he needed to.

Owen shoved his hands into his pockets. "What was he doing in the car barn?"

"He works on his motorcycle."

Owen frowned. "That piece of junk his grandpa left him? I forgot it was in there."

Eden studied him a moment. "It's his prize possession. He said working on it with his grandpa was his fondest memory as a young man."

Owen was silent as they watched Lucy and Blake kick the purple-and-pink ball around the yard. Cuddles joined in as well. Eden chuckled at the cute picture they made. Even with his stiff leg, Blake made a valiant attempt to return the ball in Lucy's direction.

"Does Lucy have any memory of my son?"

Caught off guard by the question, Eden took a moment to measure her words. "No. Not really. I show her his picture and tell her about him, but she was only three when he died."

"Did my son play with her?"

She knew what he was really asking. He wanted to know if Lucy would have cherished memories the way Blake did. Her heart broke for him. "Mark would read her a book each night before bed when he was home. They enjoyed eating ice cream together." It was a pitifully short list. "Mark adored her." She touched his shoulder, compelled to speak her mind. "Owen, Blake is your son, too. He's a good man. He was a police detective. He helped people. He's kind and thoughtful and he has a big heart."

Owen nodded, then turned and left the room, leaving her wondering what was nagging at his mind.

Blake's heart was a tangled mess of emotions when he walked into Lucy's classroom the next day. He was filled with pride over his adorable niece, but tense about filling his brother's shoes. How did a dad act at one of these things? Hopefully, watching the other fathers would give him a clue.

"Uncle Blake!"

Lucy scurried from her chair and raced toward him. He scooped her up and gave her a hug.

"Come see my desk."

Lucy proudly showed off her chair and her crayons and all her other school supplies until the teacher announced that it was time to go to the lunchroom. The cafeteria smelled like hot dogs and cake, just as he remembered. Some things never changed. After filing through the food line, they took a seat at tables and chairs that were not designed for a grown man. He was listening to Lucy's chatter when a hand touched his shoulder.

"Never expected to find you here."

Blake smiled as he recognized Norman's voice. "Same here."

Norman took a seat beside him. "This is Sadie, my middle one."

Lucy smiled. "Sadie is my best friend."

Blake chuckled. Lucy had introduced him to a dozen little girls she claimed were her "bestest friends."

"I was going to call you this afternoon. We have a problem at the office. Can you swing by when we're done here?"

"Sure. It sounds serious. What's up?"

"I'm afraid the end is in sight."

Blake's enjoyment of the lunch dimmed. Thankfully, once the meal was eaten and the principal thanked all the grown-ups, he was free to leave. But not before getting a hug around his neck and a kiss from Lucy.

He and Norman arrived at Sinclair Properties at the same time and entered the office together.

Norman quickly filled him in. "The bottom line is, if we don't replace all the AC units in the Grove Hill Mall, the tenants are threatening to withhold payment until repairs are made."

"How much will it cost?"

"You have six figures lying around you don't need?"

"Ouch. Sorry. I'm on a police pension." Blake envisioned the twenty-unit complex Sinclair Properties had owned and managed for as long as he could remember. "Can we make repairs?"

"We have been but it's to a point that won't work. One of the things Mark did when he was trying to fix his mistake was change contractors. The one he hired is useless, and as a result, we've been delivering shoddy repair work to our clients. And it's finally caught up with us. I've tried getting a bank loan but we're a bad risk right now. I don't even have a rich grandpa to call on."

Blake's mind did a quick spin as an idea formed. "How much do you need exactly?"

Norman quoted the cost of replacing all the units. Blake smiled and pushed up from his chair. "I might have a solution. Give me a couple of days."

"What are you going to do?"

"Break up with an old girlfriend."

Eden turned out the lights in the museum and glanced around. It had been a long day with little accomplished. Blake wasn't here today. She hadn't expected to miss him. He'd left her a text yesterday that he'd be unable to help this weekend. She been irked that he hadn't said what he'd be doing, but then, he had a right to lead his own life and not report to her.

She was glad to see Jackie in the kitchen when she arrived home that afternoon. "Do you know where Blake is?" She tried to keep her tone even and not show too much interest in his whereabouts.

"Oh, he's out of town for a few days. He told me he had personal business to take care of. He's hoping to be back Sunday night."

"What kind of personal business?" And why did she feel left out?

"He didn't say. He looked really happy when he told me. Maybe he's met a girl."

Eden set her jaw. "I wouldn't put it past him."

Jackie turned and looked at her, a frown on her brow. "Would it bother you if he'd found someone?"

Eden turned away and started rinsing the head of lettuce. "Don't be silly."

"Funny, but I had a feeling you were starting to have tender feelings toward our prodigal."

"You're wrong. Besides. Even if I did, which I *don't*, he's my brother-in-law. That would be out of line."

"Why?"

"I'd feel like I was betraying Mark. Falling for his brother seems so sordid."

"Maybe it would if Mark were still here, and you were cheating on him behind his back."

"Are you saying I shouldn't honor my husband's memory?"

"No. But you're still young and you have a child to raise. Turning your back on love because they were related is a bit drastic. What if you started to care for someone who was a total stranger? Someone you didn't know anything about. Would you admit your feelings then?"

"Of course not. But Blake is family."

"Not your family. He was a stranger when he showed up here. You'd never met him and the only thing you knew about him was a load of bad things that his family fed you."

Jackie came to her side and slipped an arm around her waist. "I know what I see on your face when you look at him. I hear what's in your voice when you talk about him. It's time you started to pay attention to yourself."

Eden shook her head but she couldn't get the woman's comments out of her mind.

Lucy came into the sitting area dragging her teddy bear and looking lost. "Mommy, where's Uncle Blake? I miss him."

Eden pulled her daughter onto her lap. "I know, sweetheart. He'll be back soon but you couldn't play outside. Look, it's raining. Why don't we make cookies?"

Lucy pouted but nodded. "Okay. Then can we play Barbies?"

Eden chuckled. "Yes, of course. Now, what kind of cookies should we make…?"

Her thoughts were all in a different direction as she mixed up the batter for cookies. She missed Blake, too. She enjoyed seeing him and Lucy play soccer in the yard. He was much more athletic than Mark had been. There were so many differences between the brothers it was puzzling at times.

Maybe, that was because they *were* two different men. When she looked at things logically, the only thing Mark and Blake had in common was blood and a name. If that were true, then how would that affect her growing feelings for her brother-in-law? She was attracted to him. It was hard not to be. He had a way of making her laugh and smile, he showed an interest in her and listened to her concerns. She'd been telling herself she was lonely and simply drawn to a man who showed her some attention. She knew now that she'd been lying to herself. But each time she enjoyed his company, she always came away feeling guilty.

What did she do about that?

Chapter Ten

Blake folded up the tarp Monday morning and shoved it into one of the cubbies on the wall. Working on Roxy had left a mess in the barn, and he needed to clean it up. He could hear his mother fussing about leaving his things all over creation.

He smiled. He'd used those words at Lucy the other day when she'd scattered all her yard toys around the grass. His niece had taken to following him around, but he'd told her to not go into the car barn without an adult. There were too many things that could hurt her. She'd crossed her little heart and promised, but he still kept a watchful eye on her. She was a speedy little critter.

He scanned the work area, satisfied he'd put it all in order. He had a twinge of regret letting Roxy go, but it was for a worthy cause, and it might be years before his leg was able to straddle a bike.

"Uncle Blake."

He stopped and listened. Was that Lucy? The call came again, louder and with a twinge of fear.

"Uncle Blake."

It sounded like Lucy, but she shouldn't be in the barn. Curious, he walked to the front of the building that used to be the storage space for the old cars. Before that it had been a true barn with a hayloft in the rafters.

"Uncle Blake. I'm scared."

He looked up and saw Lucy in the loft peering over the top of the ladder fourteen feet off the ground. She looked terrified. Her blue eyes were wide, and her lower lip poked out. Blake's heart stopped beating. If she fell from that height, it could be disastrous. He tried to stay calm. "How did you get all the way up there, Princess?"

"I climbed. But I can't get down. Come and get me."

Blake's blood turned to ice. He cursed his bum leg. There was no way he could maneuver the ladder with one leg and still bring the child down safely. He needed help, but he couldn't leave her and his phone was still in the workshop room. "Lucy, just sit still, okay? Stay away from the edge."

"I want my mommy."

Blake searched frantically for a solution. "Okay, I'm going to call her. Don't move." The main door was only a few yards away. He could still see Lucy and maybe shout for help. Uttering a silent prayer, he inched toward it, keeping his eyes on the child. Then, to his relief, he heard Eden calling for his niece.

"Eden. Come here, please."

She came toward him smiling but he stopped her at the door. "We have a problem."

"Mommy! I'm scared." Tears were streaking Lucy's face and sobs shook her little body.

Eden looked up and breathed out a cry of alarm. "Oh no. I'm here, Lucy."

The little girl had leaned forward, reaching out for her mother. Eden held up her hands. "No, Lucy, don't move, sweetheart. Scoot back from the edge for Mommy, okay?"

"I want to come down."

Eden hurried to the ladder, then looked at him expectantly. Blake knew she assumed he'd climb up and bring her down. His stomach lurched. He was failing her and Lucy. The two women he cared most about. He met her gaze, then tapped his leg. "I can't climb a ladder, Eden."

He saw her turn pale, then her expression filled with horror. "How can we get her down? No one's here but you and me."

Blake hated what he was about to say but there wasn't another solution. "You'll have to go up and bring her down."

"No!" She backed away. "I can't. You know I can't."

Blake took her shoulders in his hands. "You *can*. I'll talk you through it... I promise."

Trembling, she shook her head.

"Mommy." Lucy reached out her arm, stretching over the edge.

Eden tensed. "Don't move, Lucy. Sit still. Please." She looked at him, her eyes pleading. "Isn't there another way down?"

"Unfortunately, no."

"Mommy!"

Blake's heart was racing and his spirit was being shredded. Lucy was growing more panicked. They needed to get her down quickly.

"Eden, you can do this. I'll be here. I'm afraid she might get too close to the edge."

She placed her hands on her cheeks. "But I—"

He gave her shoulders a gentle shake. "There's no other choice." He was relieved to see realization form in her blue eyes. "I believe in you."

Eden looked up at her daughter, who was sobbing. "I'm coming, Lucy."

Blake turned toward the ladder, staying close. "I'll walk you through each step and I'll be here to catch you if you fall. I may have a bum leg but my arms aren't broken."

She swayed and for a moment he feared she'd pass out. "Eden?"

She cringed, then bowed her head in defeat and turned away. "I...*can't.*"

Dread swept through him. If he couldn't get her to try, he'd call the fire department, but even the few minutes they took getting here might be too long.

Eden looked up at her daughter and her vision blurred. Her baby was in danger, and she had to save her. She looked at the old wooden ladder attached to the post. It went straight up with narrow and very old slats for rungs.

She closed her eyes and groaned. *Lord, help me. I'm so scared.*

Blake took her hand and led her the few steps to the ladder. "You can do this. I'll be right here."

"Mommy." Lucy's cries suppressed some of her terror. She took hold of the sides of the ladder, fighting nausea. Eden tried to swallow but her throat was closed up. She shook her head, then felt Blake close behind her. His hand on the small of her back gave her comfort and a measure of courage.

He whispered in her ear, "Lucy needs you."

She looked up the length of the ladder. It was a long way up. Her body tensed.

"It's just a hayloft, Eden, not a Ferris wheel."

She closed her eyes, then placed her foot on the first rung, aware of Blake close at her back. "I'm coming, sweetheart."

"Keep your eyes on each rung as you go, Edie. One hand, then the other. One foot, then the other."

She took one more step, then glanced down and froze. But Blake's calm, steady voice pierced her paralysis.

"Don't look down. Keep going. You're halfway there."

Eden forced her gaze to Lucy, who was watching her anxiously, tears on her cheeks and two fingers in her mouth. She always did that when she was scared.

One more step. Reach and step. Reach and step. She realized with a jolt that she was at the top. But now what did she do? "Blake?"

"I'm right here. Take one more step, then crawl onto the loft and catch your breath. You did great."

Eden did as she was told, and the instant she settled on the rough floor, Lucy crashed into her arms. "It's okay, baby. I'm here. You're okay..."

But she knew they *weren't* okay. They still had to get down. How were they going to manage that? She looked down at Blake, who was looking up at her and smiling. As if reading her mind, he started giving her directions on how to get down.

"Eden, you need to help Lucy get onto the ladder and start down."

She didn't want to do what he said, but they couldn't stay up here. She pried her daughter's arms from her neck. "It's okay, sweetheart. You can climb down that old ladder. You're part monkey, remember? And Uncle Blake is there to catch you if you fall. See how strong he is?"

Blake flexed his arms to demonstrate.

Lucy slowly turned around and put her foot on the first rung.

Eden watched with her heart in her throat. It was up to Lucy now. There was nothing Eden could do from up here. She prayed Blake could catch her baby if she fell. Lucy moved slow and steady with Blake speaking to her all the way. He plucked her off the ladder as soon as he could reach her. The little girl clung to him, hugging his neck. Eden wished she was in that position.

Blake set Lucy down and turned his attention toward her. "Your turn, Madam Curator."

Knowing Lucy was safe had allowed her old fear to flood back into her mind, along with the nausea in her stomach. She stared at Blake. He was so far down.

"Eden, please. I can't help you climb down, but I'm here to catch you if you fall." He patted his shoulder. "Muscles, remember. But you're not going to fall. Show Lucy how brave you are."

It was the perfect encouragement. She didn't want her child to think she was afraid. She turned and reached out her foot for the first rung but couldn't find it. She yelped and froze.

"Try it again, Edie. Just an inch more and you'll touch it."

Eden glanced down and saw Lucy. She was smiling. If a five-year-old could do it… She trained her gaze on the loft and reached for the rung again. One by one, with each step conquered, Blake muttered encouragement. When she saw a horse stall between the rungs, she knew she was close.

Two more. One. Her foot touched solid ground and her knees started to buckle. Blake caught her around her waist and gathered her into his arms.

"I knew you could do it! You've conquered your fear of heights."

She shook her head. "No…not really."

He held her tighter. "I'm proud of you."

Her heart thudded, but it was a different beat from the drumming of fear. Lucy grabbed her around her knees. Eden picked her up and hugged her fiercely. "You and I are going to have a long talk about climbing things."

"Okay, Mommy."

She set her down and took her hand.

Blake took Lucy's other hand and they started toward the house. "Well, all I can say is I've never seen such brave ladies. I'm feeling pretty useless right now."

Eden looked at him, holding his gaze. "Don't. You were more help than you know."

"I think this calls for a celebration. How about some ice cream?"

"Blake, we'll be eating supper shortly," she protested.

"All the more reason to celebrate. Dessert before supper."

She wasn't going to press the point. All that mattered was Lucy was safe and Blake had made it happen. She'd be forever grateful.

Blake entered the studio and clasped his hands behind his neck. He'd escaped Eden's and Lucy's company as soon as possible. His adrenaline had faded quickly, leaving him tense and drained. The ice cream had tasted like sand in his mouth.

He sank into the recliner, massaging his forehead in an attempt to ease the pounding headache in his skull. Never had he ever felt so useless, or so worthless, than when he realized that Lucy needed him and he couldn't rescue her. He'd hated forcing Eden to go up the ladder, but he was incapable. Not even during the worst of his rehab had he ever felt so powerless. He was a cop, but he was incapable of saving the two people he loved most. The thought of losing them had shredded his heart.

He'd have to keep a closer eye on Lucy. He hadn't realized how quickly little ones could get into trouble.

Blake closed his eyes. The bigger issue was what the incident had revealed. He could no longer deny his feelings for Eden. All he wanted to do was keep her safe, make her happy and spend the rest of his life at her side.

Lord, why did You place this amazing woman in my path when I can't have her?

He jerked when his cell phone rang. He was surprised to see Eden's name on the screen. His heart jumped. Had something happened to Lucy?

"Blake, I'm sorry to bother you but Lucy won't go to sleep until you tuck her in. Would you come over and tell her good-night?"

Relief coursed through his veins. "I'll be right there."

He started across the yard, not sure if he was feeling flattered because Lucy wanted to tell him goodnight, or nervous because once again, he was assuming the role of parent, the job that belonged to his brother.

Eden greeted him at the door. "I'm sorry. She just

won't lie down unless you're here. I hope you don't mind."

"Of course not. She's my little buddy." He looked into her blue eyes and added silently that she was the woman he loved.

He followed Eden upstairs to Lucy's room, drinking in a feast of girlie, ruffled curtains, pink-and-purple bedcovers, frilly dolls and a few pieces of sports equipment for good measure. He smiled. It was exactly what he would have expected from the little princess.

"Uncle Blake. I wanted to tell you good-night." She held out her arms and he sat on the edge of the bed and accepted her hug. "Good night, Lucy." He held up his fist and she popped her small one against it. "You were very brave today, coming down that ladder."

His niece glanced at her mother. "I'm not going to climb it again."

"Good to hear. You scared us a big bunch."

Lucy smiled at him. "But you and Mommy helped me down."

Blake looked at Eden. "Mommy did most of the helping. She's very brave."

Eden broke eye contact and gently pressed Lucy back down on the bed and tugged up the covers. "Now, please go to sleep."

"Okay. I love you, Uncle Blake."

Blake's heart twisted and throbbed and melted into a lump in his chest. "I love you, too, Princess."

Back downstairs, Blake made a beeline for the door. The faux-family scenario was closing in on him, stealing his breath and clouding his mind. He reached for the doorknob as Eden called his name.

"Thank you for coming. And thank you again for

helping me and Lucy." She took a step toward him and gently touched his arm. "I don't think I'm over my fear of heights, but I know I can if I have to."

Blake lost himself in her blue eyes. "You're braver than you think. Brave and beautiful, and the most amazing woman I've ever known." She looked up at him, tilting her chin just so. All he had to do was kiss her. There was no way he could resist.

He took possession slowly, surprised and encouraged by her response. She melted against him and somehow his arms were around her, her hands gripping his shoulders.

Realization slammed into his mind at where he was heading. "Eden, I shouldn't have. I didn't mean… Good night."

He turned and walked out, taking refuge in the studio. He might be able to put walls and locked doors between him and Eden, but he couldn't find any barrier that would keep her out of his mind and heart.

What kind of man did that make him? A weak one who had fallen for his brother's wife.

Eden pulled up at the museum a few days later and found Owen's car parked near the door. A rush of dread touched her heart. "Oh no. More stuff." She regretted her words as she went to the door. She loved her father-in-law, but his constant criticism of her efforts was wearing thin.

She expected to find Owen in the main room, but it was empty. He wasn't in the storage room or the office or in the yard out back. As she walked back through the church, she noticed the door to the sanctuary was open. She peeked in and saw him seated in the front pew, staring at the pulpit and the large cross mounted on the back wall. A jolt of alarm chased along her nerves. "Owen. Are you all right?" He didn't respond. "Do you need something?"

"Jackie quit."

Eden wasn't sure she'd heard him correctly. "What do you mean? Quit what?"

"Us. Me. She's walked out."

Eden struggled to understand. "No. She can't quit. She's family. Why would she leave us?"

"Me. She left *me*."

The dejection in Owen's voice broke her heart. She sat down beside him and put her hand on his arm. "What happened?"

"She said she was tired of trying to climb over my wall of pride." He raised his chin. "She's like my wife."

Eden was more confused than ever. Only one thing was clear. "Call her, apologize, do whatever you have to do, but convince her to come back. She's family, she belongs here with us." Owen continued to stare at the altar without responding.

A thought suddenly intruded into her confusion. Lucy. If Jackie was gone, then someone had to pick her little girl up from school in…she checked her watch… ten minutes. Hurrying to the office for some privacy, she punched in Blake's number to her phone. "Blake, we have a problem. Owen is here at the museum—"

"Let me guess, he has more important things for you to add to the shelves."

"No. Blake, I found him just sitting in the sanctuary staring. He told me Jackie has quit."

"*What?* Are you joking?"

"No. I tried to find out what happened but he's not making sense."

"I'll be right over."

"No, wait. I need you to pick up Lucy from school. It was Jackie's day to do that. Take her home and I'll be there as soon as I can. I want to sit with Owen for a while."

When she rejoined her father-in-law, he was standing at one of the stained glass windows. She debated whether to speak to him. "Owen?"

Slowly, he turned and faced her. His eyes were filled with sorrow, his shoulders slumped. Her heart ached. He looked older, tired and defeated. She'd never seen him like this. She started toward him, but he met her gaze.

"You go on. I want to stay here awhile. I need to think."

"Are you sure?"

He nodded and looked away. Reluctantly, Eden went to her car and slid behind the wheel. She wanted to cry. She needed Blake. They had to sort this thing out.

Her thoughts had been rotating over and over like a taffy pull machine reliving his kiss, which had felt so right, and the guilt over letting it happen. He'd become a friend and she valued his advice but she'd allowed that to overcome her judgment.

Lucy and Blake were in the yard kicking the ball around when she arrived at Oakley Hall. The sight gave her a welcome sense of security. He was a man who would always take care of those he loved. He came toward her, his expression filled with concern. "What's going on?"

"I don't know but I'm scared. I've never seen him

like this. Blake, we have to get Jackie back. We need her."

He took her hand. "I know. She's family."

Eden had half expected him to say they needed her around the house for all the things she took care of, but he'd only thought about how much they needed her as a family member.

Her eyes filled with grateful tears. He had a kind heart. "I tried calling Jackie, but it goes to voice mail."

"Where would she go?"

"I don't know. This has been her home since she came here." Tears rolled down her cheeks. "Why would she suddenly walk out?"

Blake squeezed her hand. "I'll check with Tony. He might know what's going on. Don't worry. I'll talk to Owen, too."

He started to stand but she grabbed his arm. "Thank you. I don't know what I'd do without you here."

"I'm glad I came home so I could help."

Eden watched him walk away, struck by how much things had changed. She'd wished Blake away but now she couldn't imagine Oakley Hall without him.

When had her opinion changed?

Keeping his promise to Eden to bring Jackie back was proving to be more difficult than he'd hoped. For the last four days, his calls had gone to voice mail, and Tony had been as shocked as anyone to hear his mother had quit. He promised to look into things.

And Owen… Well, he was a closed book. The stubborn old man refused to talk about Jackie and had taken to sitting in his office.

Blake sought solace in the car barn, wishing he still

had Roxy to tinker with and keep his mind off everything else. The empty spot in the workshop mocked him. He doubted his sacrifice had made any difference. Footsteps on the wood floor drew his attention. Eden was coming toward him. He couldn't help but smile. The bright yellow sweater she was wearing made her look like a ray of sunshine walking through the dim interior. "Hi."

She smiled. "Hi. I was wondering if you'd gotten in touch with Jackie yet. I keep trying her number but no luck."

He looked at her and his heart pounded in his chest. Since the kiss, he'd been consumed with thoughts of her along with a hefty dose of guilt. She'd kissed him back, but he couldn't put too much stock in that. Eden was vulnerable after that scare with Lucy. "Uh, yeah, I talked to Tony this morning. She's in Gulfport with her daughter for a while. He said he'd call her and see if he could convince her to talk to one of us."

Eden sighed. "I miss her so much. Owen is like a statue. He just sits and stares. I found him in his office the other day staring out the window. He wouldn't even answer me when I spoke. I—"

She stopped and looked past him, her forehead creased. He braced for what was coming. "Where's Roxy?"

Blake took a nonchalant tone. "Oh, she has a new boyfriend now."

"You *sold* her? Why? I thought she was your prized possession. Your fondest memory."

He shrugged. "I have new memories now. There's a time to every purpose under heaven." He held his smile as she studied him. "I'm thinking of getting another one to restore. Something to keep me busy."

She nodded but her blue eyes were filled with doubt. "Okay. Well, if you hear from Jackie, let me know."

"Sure thing."

Eden turned and started out, then spun around. "Blake, thank you again for saving Lucy."

He shook his head. "You saved her. I just stood watch."

"You did more than that. You literally encouraged me every step of the way. I'm eternally grateful."

"It's what family members do."

"No. Not all members."

She walked out and Blake exhaled a heavy sigh. Gratitude. That's not what he wanted from Eden. But that's what he'd settle for. Nothing else was possible.

Eden had barely left the barn when his phone rang. He answered without looking at the name on the screen, expecting it to be Jackie. When he ended the phone call, he smiled. He would never stop marveling at the way the Lord worked things out. It was never the way he expected or planned, but it was always the best situation and usually from out of left field.

A swirl of excitement surged through his system, making him grin again. He had a job offer. A job with the police. There was an opening for an academy instructor at the Mobile Law Enforcement Training Center. It wasn't a desk job, either. There would be paperwork, of course, but mostly he'd be working with the cadets, teaching them the things he'd learned.

Blake glanced out at the main house. He wanted to tell Eden the good news. He'd tried not to dwell too much on his future. Working at the museum, spending time with Lucy and digging through Mark's files had kept him too busy to think.

This was truly an answer to his prayers, but now it meant leaving Eden and Lucy behind and he wasn't sure how he could do that.

Eden glanced out the kitchen window later that day and saw Blake step off his porch and out onto the lawn. His limp was obvious today. That usually meant he'd overdone things. Probably playing with Lucy again. Their ball games were always fun to watch and her little girl looked forward to them, but she suspected they took a physical toll on Blake. Each time she saw him with Lucy she hoped his leg would improve over time so he could actually run and play and not have to always use his cane for support.

On impulse, she went outside and intercepted him on his way to the car barn. "Hello, Blake."

He turned and smiled. The look on Blake's face should have been her first clue. She'd never seen him so happy. "You're in a good mood."

"Yes I am. I just got offered my dream job. I never imagined something like this would come along."

Eden couldn't help but revel in his exuberance. There had been little joy in his life since coming home, and he deserved to be happy, but an uneasy feeling settled in her chest. "Where will you be working?"

He set his hands on his hips and expanded his chest. "I'm going to be an instructor of academy cadets at the Mobile, Alabama, training center." He came toward her. "It's perfect. Not too much desk work and lots of time working with the trainees. I didn't think I'd ever get to work in law enforcement again, other than being chained to a desk."

Eden's heart burned and her throat began to close. Her worst fears had been realized. She set her jaw and crossed her arms over her chest. "So, you're leaving?"

"I guess so. They want me as soon as I can report."

Her initial excitement was quickly turning to anger. "What about the museum? And the bicentennial?"

"Well, I suppose…"

"And your father, and the company?" She choked back tears. She would not let him see her cry. "And what about Lucy? She'll be heartbroken."

"It's not like I'm moving to Dubai. I'll come and visit."

"I should have known you'd revert to your old ways."

A muscle ticked in his jaw. "Meaning?"

"Turning your back on your family when they need you most."

"No. It's not like that. The bicentennial will happen if I'm here or not. The museum is all but ready to open, such as it is." He swallowed. "As for my dad, he's made it clear from the get-go that I wasn't to get involved with his business. He won't be sad to see me go."

"That's not true. He's mentioned you several times. I think he is starting to change his mind about things."

"Not likely," he muttered.

Eden backed away, her emotions threatening to explode at any moment. "I knew you showing up here was a bad idea." She spun around and hurried back inside the house, her vision a watery blur. Seeking refuge in her room, she curled up in the window seat, her heart in shreds. Blake was leaving. She wasn't surprised. She'd been balancing her emotions for a long time, wondering when he'd display his true colors. She should have realized when he sold Roxy that he was preparing to cut ties to the Sinclair family. Walking away from her and Lucy.

A sob caught in her throat. Foolishly, her heart had begun to believe that the real Blake was the one she'd come to know and love these last weeks. Love? How had she allowed this to happen? When had Blake burrowed into her heart and past all her defenses?

A wave of guilt washed through her. But she wanted him to be happy and this job was perfect for him. If only it were here and not in another state.

Wiping tears from her cheeks, she looked out the window, her gaze finding the studio. She'd come to depend on him being there and seeing him every day. Maybe with him gone, her feelings would change. Perhaps it wasn't love but only infatuation.

Hugging her knees, she bit her lip. No. What she felt was more than attraction, but along with that came the guilt over him being Mark's brother.

She had no idea how to sort out her tangled emotions.

Eden had found no answers to her conflicting feelings as she left the grocery store later.

"Eden."

She turned at the sound of her name and saw Norman Young coming toward her across the parking lot. She smiled. "Hello. Good to see you. I hear you had a fun time at the school lunch."

Norman smiled. "We did. Blake seemed to enjoy playing parent."

She sighed. Apparently not enough to hang around.

"I have to tell you, Blake has been a real blessing

since he returned. It's a shame Owen can't see what he's done. Don't know what makes the man so bull-headed."

"What do you mean?" she murmured.

"Thanks to him Sinclair Properties can survive awhile longer. If he hadn't sold that motorcycle of his, we'd be in bankruptcy right now."

"I don't know what you're talking about."

"That old bike of his. Who knew it was worth six figures. He got top dollar for it at the auction in Nashville last weekend."

Eden's mind was churning with questions. "He sold Roxy to save the company?"

"Yeah, didn't he tell you?"

"No."

She mulled over the things Norman had told her as she drove home, trying to sort through the information. Had Blake really sold his beloved bike to save his family business? Did Owen know? The one time Blake had suggested helping at the office, his father had exploded. Had Blake ignored the warning?

The way she was ignoring her feelings? How did she reconcile her guilt with her affection? How and when had it happened? She thought back and saw a trail of little things that had led her to this point. Blake's attention to Lucy and his willingness to always help. He hated history but he'd been at the museum every time she'd needed help. He'd even taken over on several occasions.

Then there was his kindness and understanding when they first visited Beaumont, and his comfort when it had been destroyed. And his strength in helping her and Lucy from the loft couldn't be discounted. But all of that didn't change the fact that he was her husband's brother, and her first loyalty was to Mark.

Wasn't it?

Chapter Eleven

Blake closed the small journal, his emotions a familiar mix of anger and sorrow. His father had always been a manipulator, skilled at getting others to do what he wanted, but he never expected Owen to be so selfish that he'd press his own son to take any risk necessary to grow his business.

He stared at the thin gray journal on the table. That one small book had answered all his questions about Mark, his dad and the crisis at the family business. Now, what did he do with that information? If he was leaving Blessing for Mobile, then he couldn't, in good conscience, keep what he'd discovered from Eden and his dad.

He'd imagined every scenario of his revealing the truth about his brother. The fallout could be huge, or it could finally answer so many questions both Eden and his dad had about why Mark had made some of the decisions he had.

Eden was expecting him to leave. He doubted that telling her the truth would make him any worse in her eyes. Eden was obsessively loyal to her husband, so this news wouldn't dent her image of him for long. She was the type that would hold fast to the good memories and excuse the bad.

Owen was another matter. Exposing his role in this situation could go many different ways. Most likely Blake would be banned from Oakley Hall again, this time for life. The shock of what Mark had done and why could set off the granddaddy of all tirades. Or it could bring about another heart attack.

By the time dawn had made an appearance, Blake had reached his decision. First thing was to tell Eden and judge her reaction. Then worry about telling his father later. Blake had no idea how Eden would react. Anger, disappointment, shock, maybe even relief. Most assuredly she'd hate him for digging up the facts.

Maybe the bright spot in all of this was that it would place a wide barrier between them. Neither of them could come to terms with their feelings with Mark's memory looming over their shoulders. It was an impossible situation.

Blake stepped into the kitchen of the main house and found Eden in her favorite spot on the small sofa in the sitting area. "Morning." For a moment he feared she'd ignore him. News of his job hadn't been received well. He breathed a sigh when she finally met his gaze.

"Come for more coffee?"

He slipped his hands into his jeans pockets. "No. I thought you might like to take a walk around the grounds. It's a really nice morning." The suspicion in her eyes nearly sabotaged his plan.

"Okay. But what's wrong?"

"I need to talk to you privately. It's about Mark." Her

expression closed up and he feared she'd refuse to come with him. "It's important. And for your ears only."

"All right." She slipped on a light sweater as she came toward him. "You're scaring me."

"I don't mean to, but I have information you might want to hear."

They strolled toward the back of the three-acre lot in silence. Finding the courage to tell her was harder than he'd expected. "I've been puzzled by many of the decisions Mark made the last years of his life. It didn't make sense. My brother was a solid, controlled, detail-oriented man."

"I know."

He took a deep breath. "I started looking into his papers and the files left in the studio."

Eden glared at him. "You went through his personal things?"

"Not at first. I just looked at the business documents and I found the purchase agreement for the Meridian company. That was the start of everything falling apart. Then I examined his date book, and his journals."

"What journals?"

"He started keeping one shortly before he bought the Meridian company."

"You read his diary?" she spat. "All his deepest private entries? You're despicable. That's low even for you."

He winced at her accusations. "Probably but I had to understand what happened."

"And what did you find?"

"Mark was pressured into buying that business," he told her. "Owen practically ordered him to grow the company or he'd be replaced."

"That's ridiculous. Owen would never fire Mark."

"No, I don't believe he would. But he wasn't above threatening and coercing to get what he wanted, and Owen wanted Sinclair Properties to be a bigger fish in a bigger pond." He released a harsh breath. "And he put all his manipulative skills to work on Mark to make it happen."

"No. Owen wouldn't do that."

His tone softened. "I don't think he meant to, Eden, but it's his way. He sees his criticism and pushing as a way to get people to achieve their full potential, and Mark fell into the trap."

"No," she said thickly. "Mark had a tumor. He was sick and he wasn't thinking clearly…"

"All that's true, but it all started with Owen's pressure to grow the company. I think the pressure became so fierce that he did what Owen wanted only to realize that he'd sealed the company's fate. I think that's when he started gambling."

Eden had her arms wrapped around her waist, clearly distressed at what he was telling her.

"Mark wrote how he went to a conference in a Biloxi casino," Blake continued. "And he decided to try his hand at the games, and he won. Big. He thought, if he could win enough money, he'd be able to save the company and grow it at the same time and make Dad happy."

"Are you saying my husband was to blame for the company's troubles?"

He stopped and faced her. "Mark was desperate to save it in any way he could. He wrote about his frustration and his sense of failure for letting Owen down. He deeply regretted his separation from you and Lucy.

He planned to make it up to you once he got things back on track."

"But he didn't."

"No. He found out about the tumor around that time, and it made him more determined to get things right. I think from then on, the tumor was distorting his thought process and there was nothing he could do."

"Why didn't he tell me he was sick?" she cried. "I could have helped."

"He said he wanted to spare you the pain and sorrow."

Eden turned away. "What kind of man doesn't tell his wife he's dying? And Owen, why would he drive his son to make such a reckless decision?"

Blake had no answers.

"Why didn't he tell me? I could have helped somehow. I would have understood his isolation, helped shoulder his burden. Isn't that what wives are for?" She covered her face with her hands. "How could he be so selfish?"

"He was trying to protect you."

She spun around and faced him, eyes shooting daggers. "That's the Sinclair way, isn't it? To go it alone, keep it all inside. Pursue your way no matter what." She lifted her chin. "That's what you did, too, isn't it? Your way was to be a cop instead of standing by your family."

"Eden—"

"Now you get to do it again. Ride off to Mobile and leave the rest of us to clean up the mess."

He clenched his jaw. "I thought you had a right to know the truth about what Mark was going through."

"Thank you for opening my eyes. Now I can sleep

easy knowing my husband shut me out of his pain and sickness because he didn't want me to worry. And my father-in-law drove his son to the brink of disaster for his big dream." She turned away again, but muttered under her breath, "I deeply appreciate your shattering my image of my family."

The sarcasm and hurt in her tone sliced through him. "Eden, that wasn't my intention."

She was striding toward the house and didn't look back.

Now she could add his name once again to her hate list. Instead of seeking her input about delving into his brother's past, he'd taken matters into his own hands, assuming that she'd be relieved when she learned the truth.

Eden was right. He should never have come home.

Eden's blood was still boiling later that day. Blake's "helpful" revelations had unleashed all her old anger at Mark and piled on resentment toward Owen. No. He hadn't stirred it... He'd dug it up. She'd buried all those old feelings deep and staunchly refused to examine them.

Now she had no choice.

She glanced at the clock. Time to start supper but she had no idea what to prepare. She'd seriously considered ordering pizza, but Owen was not a fan. Maybe he'd agree to takeout from his favorite restaurant. She was in no mood to cook.

Without Jackie to oversee meals, this last week they hadn't been eating as well. Owen hardly touched his food. She couldn't decide if it was her cooking or just that he missed Jackie.

"Mommy. I'm hungry. Can I have macaroni and cheese for supper?"

"I have a better idea. Why don't we eat out tonight. I was going to ask grandpa where he'd like to go. Want to come with me?"

"Okay."

She started down the hallway as Owen stepped from his office. He was holding his chest.

"I need…help."

"Owen!"

She quickly helped him to a chair and pulled out her phone. "Lucy, run and get Uncle Blake. Tell him Grandpa is very sick."

The next several minutes were a blur of fear and worry and confusion waiting for the ambulance, and watching Owen being carried off to the hospital. Blake had been her rock and helped her sort out what she should do next. He sent her on to the hospital and took Lucy to Addie's.

Now she sat in the ER waiting room, terrified of losing her father-in-law. He was the father she never had. Her tension eased greatly when she saw Blake coming toward her. For the first time she fully understood that Blake wasn't the man she expected, but after what she'd learned about Mark, neither was he. She'd begun to wonder if deep down Owen wasn't who he tried to be, either.

"Any news? How is he?"

"The good news is that it wasn't a heart attack. They think it was anxiety. He's stabilized but they're going to run tests and keep him here a few days for observation."

Blake exhaled a tense breath and bowed his head. "I was afraid I'd be too late. I was afraid he'd be..."

Eden touched his shoulder and he slipped his arm around hers, then she rested her head against him a moment.

Blake looked down at her. "I called Jackie. She's on her way."

Eden breathed an audible sigh of relief. "Good. He'll be glad to see her. I think he missed her more than he let on."

The doctor came out and spoke to them, assuring them that Owen was being moved to a room and would be resting the rest of the night. He encouraged them to go home.

Eden shook her head. "No. I'm not leaving. Someone should be here with him."

"All right. I'll stay, too."

Eden took Blake's hand. "Thank you." He smiled and her heart skipped a beat. "We might be in for a long night."

"I know. I kind of like the idea."

She smiled and settled in beside him. In fact, she'd like to be at his side forever.

Blake yanked his phone from his pocket the next morning when it rang, expecting to see the name of the hospital, not Norman's name. "Hey, what's up?"

"I thought I should tell you right away about some changes that have occurred."

Blake braced himself. "Okay."

"I've been offered a job in New Orleans. It's a great opportunity and I can't turn it down. Sorry to leave you in the lurch right now but I have to let them know tomorrow."

Blake rubbed his forehead. Just once he'd like to get good news. "I understand. I appreciate you letting me know. How soon will you leave?"

"Two weeks. The thing is, who's going to take the reins here? I was hoping you could convince Owen to come back."

"Owen's in the hospital. He suffered some kind of attack yesterday. He's not in any shape to run the business." Norman was quiet a moment.

"I'm sorry to hear that. But, maybe another Sinclair could step up to the plate. Having you associated with the business would go a long way to restoring clients' confidence. The only other option is to sell Oakley Hall."

"No. That's out of the question."

Blake's insides were being squeezed like a vise. He never wanted the company, never wanted to work there. Now he was faced with running the whole show. It was the last thing he wanted to do, especially with his dream job within his grasp. But he couldn't let his family home be sold to save a dying company. Not now that his dad was ill. In all the years he'd been gone he'd never considered that his father wouldn't be there, giving orders, being in charge. But seeing him in the hospital bed frail and weak had forced him to face the truth.

Time was running out. It was up to him now. Eden's words rang in his ears. *Running away. Turning his back. Rejecting his family.* Maybe she was right. Maybe, in his own way, he was as selfish and bull-headed as his father. Maybe he'd been running all his life from the thing he was destined to do. He'd come home to repair his relationship with Owen and to make amends. What better way than to step in and save the business that meant so very much to him?

"Blake? You still there?"

"Yeah. I'm here." He blew out a long breath. "Looks like I'm going to be here for a long time."

"Does that mean you'll come and run the business?" Norman asked.

"Yeah."

"Friend, I know this isn't something you're thrilled with. But, in all honesty, I think you'll do a wonderful job."

Blake hung up the phone, his heart like lead in his chest. The only small ray of hope was that Eden might be happy that he was staying to help the family.

But first he had a call to make and a job to turn down.

Blake stepped into his father's hospital room the next day to find Jackie at Owen's side and Eden seated in a bedside chair. She'd arrived last night and sent him and Eden home to rest.

"Good morning, Jackie. It's good to see you with the family again. You know you belong here."

Jackie scowled in Owen's direction. "It seems so. When I'm not here everything falls apart and people end up riding in ambulances."

Owen harrumphed but he had a faint smile on his face, which Blake found odd.

He approached his father. "How are you doing today?"

Owen held his gaze a moment. "Ready to go home tomorrow."

"Good." Thunder rattled the windows. "Better than trying to get home in this rain. It's supposed to get worse. They're predicting heavy downpours and high winds this afternoon."

The nurse brought Owen lunch and Eden and Blake took the time to grab a bite to eat in the cafeteria. On their way, Eden took his hand. "He's doing so much better. The doctors confirm it was an anxiety attack. It's very strange but I'm just glad he's feeling better."

"Me, too." Blake studied her a moment. Should he tell her about his decision to stay and run the company?

He paid scant attention as Eden filled him in on the tests the doctors had run and the recommendations they'd laid out. But he knew that no matter what the doctors said, Owen would do as he pleased. The man always had and always would. But he was just grateful that his dad wasn't seriously ill. He might need his help going forward.

Blake really could use Eden's support with his new decision, but he wasn't sure how she would react. He finished his drink. No. Now wasn't the time to stir up the waters. Later, when Owen was home and settled, he'd tell Eden about Norman leaving and his taking charge.

"What do you think?"

Blake jerked back to the moment and realized Eden was staring at him. "What?"

"About Owen's anxiety. What do you think could have caused it? I doubt if Jackie's leaving would have upset him that much."

He had trouble organizing his thoughts. "I don't

know. Mark was the only one who understood him. I could never figure him out."

Eden held his gaze a moment. Then she huffed out a breath of irritation and shook her head.

Obviously, he'd not responded the way she'd hoped. He watched her walk across the cafeteria and disappear into the hall before he stood and started walking back to Owen's room.

Eden wasn't in his future whether he stayed in Blessing or moved to Mobile. Not with Mark's memory between them.

How was he supposed to live with that?

Blake made his way slowly back to Owen's room, his thoughts in a jumble. The family were all staring at the television, which was tuned to the local weather report.

Jackie shook her head. "Looks like the storm is getting worse. They're predicting hurricane-force winds. Maybe you and Blake should head home." Thunder and lightning flashed and boomed overhead as rain pounded against the window. "Or maybe it's too late."

Eden whirled away from the window. "Lucy. She doesn't like to be away from home when it storms."

Blake grabbed his jacket and umbrella. "I'll get her. I'll swing by the museum first and make sure everything is secure. Eden, you stay here until the storm passes. I don't want to have to worry about you driving in this."

The rain was coming down hard when he pulled up to the museum. He picked up the potted plants near the entrance that Eden had placed there and set them inside the door. The wind was picking up and slammed the door back against the outside wall. It resisted when

he pulled it shut. He turned on the lights but before he
could walk to the middle of the room, the power went
out. Using his phone, he made a quick survey of the
windows and doors and checked the back entrance,
where a few discarded items had been left.

As he made his way back through the building, his
phone wailed with a weather warning. A quick check
told him he might not be able to make it out to the edge
of town to pick up Lucy from her friend's house. His
best plan would be to hunker down and wait it out.
He selected Eden's number to let her know about the
change in plans, but his phone lacked service.

The wind screamed overhead, and he headed to the
innermost room of the old church. As he ducked inside,
a loud crashing noise assaulted his ears. The building
shook and glass shattered.

Blake covered his head and crouched in the corner
of the room.

Eden stood staring out the hospital room window, her
thoughts a downpour of confusion. Her father-in-law
was going to be all right but what about Blake? Had this
health scare changed his mind about leaving Blessing?
She hoped so because she wanted him to stay. But she
wanted him to be happy, too.

If only there was a way to make this right for everyone. Try as she might she couldn't find a way to
make that happen.

"Eden, come away from that window. What if it
breaks in this wind?" Jackie tugged on her arm and
steered her toward the chair near the bed.

But she couldn't sit down. She was too worried
about Blake. Addie's mother had called and told her

to tell him not to come. The weather was too bad. She assured Eden that Lucy was fine. Addie's older sisters had built a blanket fort in the living room, and they were having popcorn and ice cream while they waited out the storm. If need be, Lucy could spend the night again and come home in the morning.

Eden held her phone to her ear, waiting for Blake to answer, her gaze riveted on the darkness outside. The storm was worse than they predicted, and she needed reassurance that he was safe at the church. This was her third call with no response. The worst of the storm had passed through a short while ago, but she kept getting an unavailable notice.

She heard a soft gasp from Jackie and turned to look at the older woman. Her gaze was glued to the television screen. Eden saw a video of the museum and a reporter in rain gear talking about the storm.

"Straight-line winds of over ninety miles per hour ripped through downtown Blessing, leaving destruction in their wake."

The video showed the roof being torn off the local motel and the metal canopy over one of the gas stations blowing off and twisting into a heap. The next image chilled her blood and squeezed her throat.

"The former Saint Joseph's Church took a hit when its steeple was torn from the roof and a small addition in the back of the building was demolished by a falling tree."

The video clearly showed Blake's car parked at the entrance. Eden's heart pounded and electrical jolts of fear shot through her nerves. She was faintly aware of Jackie putting her arm around her shoulders. Eden stared at the phone in her hand and tried again to call Blake.

Her knees buckled and she sank into a chair. "He was there. In the middle of it. What if…?"

"Shh. Don't think like that. They haven't mentioned anyone being inside. Let's not jump to conclusions. Blake is a resourceful guy and he's been in dozens of worse situations. I'm sure he took the right precautions."

In her heart she knew Jackie was right, but her heart also was revealing just how much she cared for Blake. She couldn't bear the thought of losing him.

"Owen. What's wrong?"

Yanked from her internal turmoil, Eden faced her father-in-law and saw an expression on his craggy features she'd never seen before. She wasn't sure how to interpret it. Shock. Horror. Grief.

"Owen, are you in pain?" Jackie asked. "Do you want me to call the doctor?"

When he didn't respond, Jackie reached for the nurse call button. He appeared quickly and made a cursory check of Owen, who kept trying to wave off the examination.

The diversion temporarily diverted Eden's emotions, but a glance at the TV brought it all back. She tried again, fighting tears and a hole in her heart that was growing by the second. She tried to ignore all the horrible scenarios that kept forming in her mind, of Blake lying unconscious on the floor or trapped under the fallen tree.

Unable to remain still, she picked up her purse and slung the strap over her shoulder. "I'm going to the museum."

"Eden, no. Stay here."

"I can't, Jackie. I have to know if he's all right."
The woman started to protest, then sighed and nodded.

"Okay, but be careful. Sounds like lots of streets are
blocked with fallen trees and power lines. Let us know
when you get there."

"Owen?" Eden asked.

"He's fine. Go."

Blake carried the wet book into the kitchen and
opened it on the table. At first glance only the top few
pages were wet. Maybe they could dry them out and
hope that the underlying pages weren't too severely
damaged.

"Blake."

He turned at the sound of his name. What was Eden
doing here? He hurried out into the main room and
was wrapped in a fierce hug. Eden clung to him like a
vine. "Why did you come? Has something happened?"

She spoke against his chest. "I was afraid I'd lost
you."

All the breath in his chest whooshed out. Had he
heard her right? Did she care that much?

He gently cradled her head with one palm. "I'm fine,
but I confess to having a moment there when the tree
fell. Sounded like a bomb going off."

She looked up at him. "How bad is it?"

"See for yourself." He walked her into the sanctuary, where the steeple had left a split in the ceiling.
"Thankfully, the hole didn't go all the way through.
A stained glass window near the entrance was shattered. The worst is in the back." He stopped at the door
to the small room that had once been a nursery. The

room was pancaked into the ground, the trunk of the tree and broken branches filling the space.

Eden moaned softly. "Oh no. This is awful. If that tree had fallen in a different direction…" She turned and looked at him, her eyes moist. "I'm glad you're safe."

"Me, too." Blake held her gaze, warmed by the softness in her eyes. He allowed himself to believe she cared for him more than just a friend or family member. She placed her hand on his cheek and slowly stroked her thumb over his skin. He sucked in a surprised breath.

"Careful, lady. You'll start giving me ideas."

"Maybe that's what I want to do," she whispered.

He smiled tenderly down at her. "I wouldn't protest."

"You wouldn't?"

"No. I care for you, Eden. A great deal. More than I should. Keep looking at me like that and I won't be responsible for my actions."

"You're always responsible, aren't you?"

"No." The temptation was too great. He lowered his head, his gaze locked on her blue eyes. She lifted her face, her hand still on his cheek. Eden whispered his name and he captured her lips. She leaned into him, returning his kiss and sending his heart rate soaring. He raised his head. "Eden, I want to tell you…"

Her eyes widened and she lifted her palm to her throat. "No. Don't."

Her cheeks were flushed as she stepped away. He held on to her arms, searching her eyes for confirmation of what they'd shared. "We need to talk about this. About what's happening between us."

"No we don't. There's nothing between us. There can't be. Ever." She turned and hurried toward the door.

He caught up with her before she could open it. "Eden, you can't keep ignoring this."

"Yes I can. I have to. For Mark."

Her words burned like a hot poker in his chest. She walked out and Blake watched her drive away in the mist.

The kiss replayed in Blake's mind a thousand times as he drove home to the studio. Eden loved him. He was certain of that. And in those few seconds, he'd seen his heart's desire. A future with Eden and Lucy. A future that could never be because neither one knew how to deal with the memory of his brother.

Blake stood on the porch of the studio the next day watching as Jackie and Eden escorted Owen into the house. Thankfully, he'd recovered quickly and had been released this morning. From where he stood, his father looked spryer than he had since Blake had arrived. Almost as if the health scare had sent him in a new direction.

Blake waited for fifteen minutes after the family had gone inside. He wanted to give Owen a chance to settle in. Then he'd assess his situation and decide whether to confront him about the pressure he put on Mark.

Eden's words came to mind. Maybe he should leave well enough alone. Maybe he should never have come home in the first place. He'd upset the applecart and accomplished nothing in the process. Worst of all, he'd never found a way to reconcile with his father.

All in all, a useless homecoming.

With the exception of meeting Eden and Lucy and losing his heart to both of them, of course. But they were Mark's family, even if Mark was no longer here.

Eden would always see him as the bad guy, the man she shouldn't care for because he was the brother.

Blake had his own reservations about that. He carried a bag of guilt for falling for his brother's wife, though technically, there was nothing wrong with them being together. On the other hand, he hated to think what Owen would say about Eden loving the wrong son.

He couldn't deny the kiss they'd shared. While they'd acknowledged their mutual attraction, the word *love* hadn't been spoken yet. He doubted it would now.

Grabbing hold of his cane, Blake went to the main house and found the family gathered in the living room. Owen looked unusually pleasant as he met his gaze. There was no fire in his eyes this time, only a question.

"I was wondering about the museum. How badly was it damaged?"

Blake winced inwardly and tried to hide his irritation. He should have known his father's first thought would be for the museum. "Bad. I've called someone to cover the holes in the roof with tarps. I'll have Eden look over the displays tomorrow and see what can be done, but it won't be open for the bicentennial if that's what you're wondering."

Owen nodded thoughtfully but didn't comment further.

Blake set his jaw. Some things never changed.

Chapter Twelve

Eden met Jackie in the hallway the next morning as she was coming down the stairs. "How's our patient this morning?"

"Surprisingly well. He seems almost contented. Though, he still doesn't like taking his medicine." She slipped her arm through Eden's. "But I have high hopes for the old goat. I think this scare might have opened his eyes to certain things."

"Like what?"

"Let's wait and see, huh? So, how are things between you and Blake?"

Eden averted her gaze. "Fine. Why wouldn't they be?"

"Any further developments on your relationship? Like maybe admissions of affection or maybe a kiss."

Her cheeks flamed. "Jackie, you are talking nonsense." She moved to the counter and started to wipe it down.

"You can deny it until your last breath, sweet girl, but we both know that you and Blake have been playing emotional dodgeball ever since the day he knocked on that back door. You can't keep your eyes off one another. Blake's heart falls out of his chest whenever he looks at you or Lucy. The man is seeing you as part of his future."

"He's not a family type of guy," Eden protested.

"Oh? Sure seems that way to me. I've seen him with Lucy. The joy on that man's face is a sight to behold. And, from what you've told me, he's been a comfort and support to you now and again."

She couldn't deny that. Despite her fierce resistance, she'd fallen in love with Blake, but it was futile. Eden could feel Jackie's gaze pinned on her back. She knew the woman too well and that she wouldn't let this rest until she got an answer that satisfied her.

Eden gripped the damp rag in her hand. "Even if you're right and there are...*feelings*...between us, it can never happen."

"Why?"

"Because of Mark. Blake is my brother-in-law. I can't fall for him."

"Why?" Jackie repeated.

"Because it's wrong. It's disgraceful. Sinful even."

Jackie grinned. "You know, in biblical times, the brother of the deceased was supposed to assume the care of his brother's family."

Eden frowned at her friend. "This isn't biblical times, and anyway, it's too soon to jump into anything."

"I wouldn't call two years jumping. Let me ask you, were you unfaithful to Mark? Did he cheat on you?"

Eden set her jaw. The woman was going too far. "No. We honored our vows."

"Uh-huh. And what is the last line of the marriage vows?"

Eden frowned. She had no idea what Jackie was leading up to. She thought about it a moment. "Uh, till death do us part."

"Exactly. You're parted. The marriage severed. The covenant fulfilled. You're free to move on to a relationship with his brother." Jackie held her gaze. "No condemnation."

"Mommy, Uncle Blake taught Cuddles a new trick. Watch."

Eden breathed a sigh of relief when Blake entered the kitchen holding Lucy in his arms with the puppy trotting along at his heels. The look of pure happiness on Blake's face brought a lump to her throat. One thing she was sure of. Blake adored little Lucy. He'd be a wonderful father.

She shut down that thought and smiled. "A new trick. Let me see it."

Blake put Lucy down and she squatted, pointing a finger at the dog. "Okay, Cuddles, show Mommy your new trick. Roll over." Lucy made circular motions with her fingers. "Roll over. You can do it."

Cuddles stared at her a moment, then sat down. Lucy looked up at her uncle. "Uncle Blake, make him do his trick."

He chuckled and leaned down. "Cuddles. Roll over." He made a quick movement with his finger and the little dog executed a perfect doggie roll. The child squealed in delight and hugged the fuzzy pup.

Eden giggled. "Good job, Lucy! That was wonderful." She looked at Blake and his gaze told her clearly that he thought she was wonderful, too. She quickly looked away.

Jackie gave Cuddles a scratch behind his ears.

"Blake, I'm glad you're here. Owen wants to have a family meeting. Might as well do it now since we're all together. I'll tell Owen."

Blake frowned and looked at her with a shrug.

"Have you ever had a family meeting before?" Eden asked.

He scratched his chin. "Never. I'm guessing he'll want to remind us to speed up the museum repairs so it will be open for the bicentennial."

"You're probably right. I can't think of anything else that would concern the family, though he has acted differently since he got home. I can't believe the change in him. It's almost like the anxiety attack has scrubbed off all his rough edges. I suppose the rest and regular medications these last few days have helped. I just hope he doesn't go back to work and put himself at risk again."

"He won't," he said.

"How can you be so sure?"

"Because he won't be the Sinclair going to the office each day," Blake told her.

Eden studied his expression. Something was wrong. She could see it in his eyes. "What do you mean?"

Blake sat down beside her. "Norman is leaving so I thought it would be a good idea to take his place and see if I can get the business back on track. I let Owen down once. I don't want to do it a second time. Not after all he's been through."

Eden touched his arm. Was he serious? "But what about your job in Mobile?"

"I turned it down. It didn't really suit me anyway. Too much time at a desk."

"You said there would be more time with trainees and—"

"I know. But I'm a Sinclair. I need to shoulder this. Besides, you were right—my coming home upset everything. That was never my intention."

Eden sighed. "Oh, Blake. I need to apologize for what I said. I was surprised, that's all. I wasn't prepared for you to go away. I was hoping…"

"What?"

"I assumed you'd stay around. Lucy likes having you here." Why was she such a coward? Why couldn't she just tell him how she felt?

"Is that the only reason?"

"I'd miss you, too."

Blake took her hand in his and gently squeezed it. "Good."

"So why are you sacrificing your future, Blake? You're not fooling me. I know how much that job meant to you. I know you never wanted to take over the company."

Eden reclaimed her hand. "I'm sorry for the way I've been acting since you came home. I always believed that if you'd joined the company, been the other son, that it would have made everything right. But I know now that I was wrong. Things wouldn't have ended differently. I think it was my way of explaining Mark's behavior." She touched his cheek. "Now I feel so sad. It's not right that you have to give up your dream for your father's."

"It's not such a sacrifice." He gazed into her eyes. "I'll be able to see you and Lucy as much as I want. That's compensation enough."

She hugged him. "You are a noble man. And I know what you did. Norman told me about your other sacrifice. I know how much that bike meant to you."

"Unfortunately, it was only a stopgap but I don't regret it. I need to stop walking away and stand and confront my demons."

Eden leaned over and gave him a brief kiss and watched the emotion bloom in his eyes. Fear and shame gathered in hers. She moved away. Soon, she'd have to make a decision about her relationship with Blake. She couldn't keep playing this yo-yo game with their feelings.

But what was the right decision? And how did she remove Mark from her thoughts without feeling disloyal?

Jackie entered the kitchen as they were ending their conversation and gave them a knowing smile. "I put Lucy down for a nap so we won't be disturbed. Owen is ready for us now." She smiled and motioned them to follow.

Blake placed a possessive hand on her arm. "So, I guess King Owen is ready to hold court."

Eden grinned. "I should have practiced my curtsy."

"Maybe a kowtow would be more appropriate."

She giggled and poked her elbow in his side.

In the living room, Owen was seated in the wing-back chair, looking every bit the king. The only odd note was Jackie, who was standing beside him with a very unusual smile on her face.

Blake and Eden positioned themselves on the sofa. Blake's chest was tight from anxiety. What could be going on? He studied his father a moment. There was a peculiar twinkle in his eyes that was unnerving. Did he have some other big scheme in mind he was going to dump on them?

Owen took a deep breath. "I asked you here to tell you about changes that I've decided to make. My recent health scare has opened my eyes to things I've been ignoring. No, that's not true. Things I chose to deny." He directed his gaze at Blake.

Blake braced for another dressing-down. What had he failed to do now?

"I've come to realize that pride and greed led me down a dead-end trail. I've done you all an injustice and I'm going to try and correct that going forward." He glanced at Jackie before continuing. "To begin with, I've arranged to have the Blessing Historical Society take over the museum. They'll pack up the contents and return them to us, with the exception of the items that generally pertain to the town's history."

Eden gasped and clutched Blake's arm. So typical. Decide but don't discuss. "Dad, Eden has worked hard getting that museum set up."

"I know and she's done a wonderful job considering the burden I placed on her shoulders. That was one of my big mistakes."

Eden exchanged a puzzled look with him. "That's very generous. I'm sure the people in this community will be grateful."

Owen nodded. "They were. I also have to admit to making a series of misjudgments over the last few years. I realize now that after my wife died, I lost my compass. She was the one who kept me from falling prey to my flaws. As a result, I've been blind and unfair to my sons. I've also taken steps to rectify that."

Eden leaned forward. "Owen, I don't understand."

"I'm in the process of finalizing the sale of Sinclair Properties to a company out of Jackson. They are a large firm, and they have a lot of experience managing small-town interests like ours."

Blake's vision blurred and his chest caved inward from the air leaving his lungs. "You sold the company?"

"It's all but a done deal."

His mind whirled. He never anticipated his father would sell out. It was *unthinkable*. He was barely aware of Eden gripping his arm.

"Owen, what will you do with your time if you're not going to go back to work?"

Jackie lowered her hand and Owen took hold of it with a smile. "I'm going traveling. Jackie and I are going to be married. We've both been alone a long time. She convinced me that it was time to turn a new page in my life and to let go of the old dreams and find new ones." He stood and pulled Jackie against his side. "I hope you'll be happy for us. And I hope you'll forgive me for being such a single-minded old—" he looked at Jackie "—goat."

Eden went to them and gave them a hug. "I'm so happy for you. I should have seen this coming." She smiled at Jackie. "You told me you were falling for the widower of an old friend. I never guessed it was Owen."

"Good. Because that would have complicated things even more."

Blake took advantage of the distraction to leave the room. He walked through the kitchen and out to the porch only vaguely aware of what he was doing. His father had just destroyed his future. He'd been unceremoniously kicked out in the cold.

Inside the studio, he ran his fingers over his scalp.

He'd spent the last few days talking himself into doing the right thing and now he'd lost it all. He wasn't needed at Sinclair Properties because it no longer existed. His job in Mobile was gone, and he had nowhere to go.

Eden. How did she fit into this new reality? He had nothing to offer her now. He had no job, security or promise of a good life ahead for her and Lucy. He'd hoped that they might start a new life together, but he couldn't take that step when he was empty-handed.

A knock sounded on the door. Eden peeked in. "Blake, I'm so sorry. I can't believe Owen is making all these changes."

She came to him and slipped her arm in his.

Blake took comfort from her nearness. "Dad has a way of pulling the rug out from under people. Like your museum."

Eden shook her head. "No. That's a relief. I've always known it was pointless. But I made a promise, and I didn't want to break it. Owen didn't know what you were planning to do. Maybe you could talk to him and he'll change his mind."

Blake shook his head. "No. It's too late. He's already set things in motion. Besides, he has a new life ahead of him. A happy life. He hasn't had that in a long time. I'm glad for him and Jackie. She'll give him the contentment he used to have with Mom. He needs a strong woman to keep him in check."

"Do you think he'll be happy traveling and not having a business to consume his time?" she asked.

Blake huffed out a skeptical breath. "I don't know. This is an Owen I've never seen before."

"Me, either. Do you have any idea what you'll do now?"

"No. I need time to think things through."

She moved in front of him, her eyes soft and brimming with affection. "You could stay here with me and Lucy."

He smiled and touched her chin. "I'm not sure that would go over well with Owen. I'd always be a reminder of the past. Not just because of being the son that failed him, but now, I'd be a reminder of my mother. He doesn't need that to complicate his new marriage. I think it's best if I just move on. Let everyone get on with their lives. I came here with nothing and I'm leaving with nothing."

"That's not true! You have me and Lucy."

"I wish that were true, but we both know that Mark's memory will always be a wall between us." His heart tightened when she didn't deny it.

"Where will you go?" she asked quietly.

"I have a friend in Nashville. I'll see what opens up from there."

Her eyes welled with tears. "Please don't go. Stay here."

"Do I have a reason?"

"Yes. Lucy loves you."

"And her mother?" he asked gruffly.

"Yes. I do. I've just been feeling so guilty. Like I was betraying Mark. But then I realized that I have a right to love again. Being a widow doesn't mean I can never feel for someone else, even my brother-in-law. Till death do us part. We're parted. I was a good wife to him. He was the best husband he could be until he got sick." She took his hand and held it to her chest. "I believed that loyalty was the most important quality. Loyal to the end. No matter what. But sometimes loyalty can make you blind. I loved Mark and I know he loved me, but he made a mistake and instead of looking for help, he tried to fix it on his own with his own power and he only made it worse. I hated him for that," she said softly.

"You did?"

"Yes," she admitted. "Until I realized I was no better. I was proud of being Mark's wife and thought I could go through life with his memory alone to sustain me." She shook her head. "But the more I saw you with Lucy, the more I came to see what kind of man you really were. I knew what I really wanted was a family again. With you. Loving you shouldn't be any different than if I met someone else who was a stranger. And you were a stranger to me. I didn't know you, only what I'd heard."

Blake pulled her into his arms. "I fell for you the moment you opened the door. I was so ashamed. It seemed so wrong and disrespectful to have feelings for my brother's wife."

"What are we going to do?"

He brushed a hair from her forehead. "What do you *want* to do?"

She stood on tiptoe and kissed him. A kiss filled with all the emotions she'd been denying. "I want a future with us together."

Blake crushed her to him, holding her close and thanking the Lord for leading him home again.

Eden stared out the window at the studio the next day. It was rainy and cold today. The kind of day you wanted to curl up with a cup of hot chocolate and a good book, or maybe a good friend. Someone you cared for.

Except Blake wasn't in the studio today. He'd left early this morning before she had to take Lucy to school. Her heart had been twisted with worry ever since. What if he didn't come back? He'd talked last night about leaving. He was right. Mark's image would always stand between them unless they could overcome their guilt.

She wished there was something she could do. He'd been blindsided. They all had, but Blake most of all. He'd been prepared to sacrifice for the company and instead he'd lost not only his position at Sinclair Properties, but his dream job in Mobile. It wasn't fair. It was wonderful that Owen had realized the error of his ways and tried to make amends, but he should have discussed things with them first, gotten their input. But that wasn't his way. Or Mark's. They'd both made decisions that affected others on their own, assuming everyone would go along.

On the other hand, Blake would never have been happy running the business given its dire condition. Someone had to do something.

Reaching her decision, Eden went in search of her father-in-law. She found him and Jackie in his study looking at the computer. He glanced up and smiled. The sight threw her for a curve. In all the years she'd known him he'd rarely smiled.

"We're researching vacation spots."

A swell of anxiety rose in Eden. Maybe this wasn't such a good idea. "I wanted to talk to you, alone, if I could."

Jackie smiled. "Of course." She kissed Owen and gently touched Eden's arm as she went by.

Her father-in-law looked at her, his bushy brows drawn together. "What is it?"

Suddenly, her courage failed. She'd never, ever questioned Owen's decisions before. Not about things in the house, or Mark or anything. She had to be prepared for him to lash out and rant again. "I need to talk to you about Blake."

"Oh. What about him?" he asked.

"There are things he's done that you aren't aware of."

The smile faded. "Do I need to call a lawyer?"

Eden filled with indignation. "Why do you always assume that he's done something wrong?"

"Well, I—"

"You've done it ever since I joined the family. Everything Blake did was wrong. You said he was reckless, heartless and dishonored his family. But you were wrong. So was Mark. I don't know what Blake did to make you so angry that you'd ban him from his home, but he's none of the things you said." She narrowed her eyes at her father-in-law. "He's a decorated police detective who has several commendations for bravery and had to resign from the force. He'll always walk with a limp."

"I—I had no idea."

"No, because you could only see your dream and Mark's role in it," she reminded him.

"I'm beginning to see that."

"I'm no better. I believed everything Mark told me. I didn't have a family role model to follow. I thought devotion to work was how my husband showed his love.

I know he loved me and Lucy, but it was love from a distance." She took a deep breath and plunged ahead. "Do you know Lucy's favorite thing to do every day? Play soccer with Blake. A man who has to use a cane to stand, but he kicks that ball to her and plays with her and loves her in ways Mark never thought of."

Owen nodded and met her gaze. "You're right. I've made every mistake a father can make. I put my dreams above everyone else's, and it caused me to lose my oldest son. Jackie has made me see things differently." He paused a moment, as if collecting his thoughts. "When we were in the hospital, and I saw that news footage of the museum and realized that Blake might be injured... that I might have lost him, too. It was like a dark cloud being lifted from my eyes. I saw clearly what I'd done, and I hated myself."

"Owen, I know you didn't mean to hurt anyone."

"No, but I was determined to achieve my goal at any cost. My wife tried to warn me but I was too prideful to listen."

Eden nodded. She knew only too well. "Owen, there's a few more things you need to know. Things Blake and Norman have been doing to try and save your company."

"What do you mean?"

"You know that motorcycle Blake inherited?" Eden shared the story behind Blake's action. "Also, did you know Norman was leaving?"

"Yes, he informed me a few days ago."

"Well, one thing you don't know is that Blake was planning on taking over, and that he turned down his dream job to try and save your business."

Owen's eyes widened. "Why would he do that?"

"Because he's a good man with a huge noble streak and a loving heart. I just thought you should know that selling the company has pulled the rug out from under him."

Eden departed Owen's office later, unsure of whether she'd made things better or worse. Her father-in-law was genuinely surprised about the things she shared with him. They talked about Mark, and she filled him in on the things Blake had uncovered. Through it all Owen had listened and nodded and stared at his hands.

He'd thanked her for telling him these things and she'd left.

She prayed she hadn't complicated things for Blake. She wasn't sure what she'd tried to accomplish, but she couldn't let his dream die without letting Owen know about his part in it.

Eden was anxious to talk to Blake and forewarn him about her talk with his father. But he'd been gone for most of the day, and it was suppertime before he returned and he didn't show up at the house to eat with the family.

She hoped Owen would go and speak with him. An honest father-and-son discussion would do wonders for their relationship. She should have known better. Owen had retreated to his study with Jackie and the pair had been secluded the rest of the day.

Eden made a point to seek out Blake early the next morning before he could get busy. The weather was still cold and drizzly, so she slipped on her heavy sweater and made her way along the covered porch to his door. He didn't answer when she knocked. Noting that his car was still parked nearby, she opened the door and called his name.

"In here."

She found him in the bedroom, stuffing his belongings into his worn duffel bag. The one he'd carried when he'd arrived. "Blake. What are you doing?"

"I'm leaving for Nashville. My friend has a job for me there."

"What? Wait, you mean you're walking out without letting me know."

He didn't respond. "Did you need something?"

"Yes. An explanation. I came to tell you I talked to Owen, and I told him what you've done to try and save the company." She held her breath, anticipating his response.

Blake glowered. "Why would you do that?"

Eden raised her chin and met his gaze. "Because he needed to know that his opinion of you was all wrong. He needed to see the full scope of his narrow point of view."

He set his hands on his hips and frowned. "What did you hope to accomplish?"

She took a few steps toward him. "I thought he might talk to you and apologize. You said you wanted to make amends. Well, you have. Several times. I wanted to see you and Owen reunited."

"That's not going to happen." Blake shoved a few more items into his duffel.

Eden's patience reached the breaking point. "Stop that." She tugged the duffel away from him. "You can't leave. We need to talk about this."

"Nothing to talk about."

She gritted her teeth. "So, you were going to just drive off with no explanation, no goodbye."

Blake exhaled loudly. "We both know it'll never

work between us. Not with Mark's shadow looming every moment. He'll always be the third person in the room."

Eden's anger caught fire. "That's a stupid excuse and you know it. This has nothing to do with Mark and everything to do with you being a Sinclair. They make a decision without consulting anyone else, without considering anyone else's feelings or opinions and just go on their way."

He avoided looking at her. "I didn't want to upset you any more than you were already."

She wanted to wring his bullheaded neck. "No. You're not getting off that easily. This wasn't about my feelings. This was all about yours and your inability to face things when they get difficult."

"Eden."

She jabbed a finger in his chest. "Mark didn't tell me about his troubles or his illness because he didn't want me to worry or cause me concern. You turned your back on your family because you didn't want to work for your dad."

"That was different."

He turned away but she forced him back around to face her. "I'm not done.

"Owen started a museum and dumped me in the middle of it. He decided that Sinclair Properties should be a big grandiose company, but he didn't bother to talk to Mark first." She took a deep breath, every nerve in her body shaking. "Then, you come along and pull me out of my shell and make me fall in love with you. But then you decide I'd be less heartbroken if you just rode off into the sunset like some cowboy in an old movie, rather than talking it over with me."

Eden crossed her arms over her chest and shook her head. "I guess I shouldn't be surprised. I've lived my adult life with the Sinclairs and I should have realized none of you are capable of putting others first. I told Mark I wanted an old home. It had been a dream of mine since I was a child. But he decided we needed something new and modern so he picked out the lot and the plan and chose all the details and then just moved me in."

"Eden, let me explain." He reached out to her.

"No. I'm finished." She raised her hands in resignation. "Go. Find your happy life in Nashville."

She spun on her heels and walked out of the studio, fighting tears as she hurried back to the main house. How could she have been so blind, so naive to think she had a future with Blake?

Jackie looked up as she entered the kitchen. "Eden, honey, what's happened? Are you all right?"

The tears she'd been fighting burst loose. "He's leaving."

Jackie gave her a hug and gently rubbed her back. "Sit down and tell me what's going on."

"I love him and he's leaving."

Blake watched Eden storm out, his heart a twisted mass of pain and regret. Dragging his hand across his face, he berated himself inwardly for his actions. Eden was right. He was acting exactly like a Sinclair. He'd made up his mind on the best course of action and proceeded to move forward without even a thought of talking to Eden first. He'd decided, on his own, that she'd be better off without him. That they could have no future together.

He sank onto the edge of the bed, his face in his hands. He wanted to talk to her and ask for forgiveness. But he'd sealed his fate. She would never listen to him now. He'd lost her trust.

How did he break the cycle? How could he prove to Eden he could change, that he *wanted* to change?

A knock on the door brought him to his feet. His heart filled with hope that Eden had returned, and he'd have a chance to explain. He opened the door to his father. The last person he wanted to see.

Blake stood his ground. "I'm kind of busy, Dad."

"I want to talk to you. It's something, well, it's long overdue."

Every instinct in him urged him to shut the door, but it was the first time his dad had ever reached out to him. He stepped back and ushered him in. "Have a seat."

Owen perched on the edge of the sofa, facing Blake as he slowly lowered himself into the recliner. Blake waited for his father to speak. When time dragged on, his irritation swelled. "Dad, I got things to do."

Owen nodded, then stared at him a long moment. "You're a lot like your mother."

"I suppose so."

"I was sorry to hear about your…leg."

Where was this going? "Well, things happen."

"Yes. Yes, they do. We aren't always prepared to deal with them."

Blake blew out an inpatient breath. "Dad, is there something you wanted to say?"

"Just that, you might not know… I mean, I didn't want to work for the company when I was younger. I wanted to be a professional golfer. I was good."

It was not what he'd expected to hear from his dad. "I thought you loved the company."

"I did. I was good at it. But no, I had other plans. Like you did. You always were brave. I wish I'd been more like you."

"You hated my rebellious ways," Blake bit out.

"No. I just didn't understand them. Not the way your mother did." Owen rubbed his hands together. "I know what you've done to help the business. The bike, giving up that job…"

"Eden shouldn't have told you."

"She was proud of you and wanted me to know what kind of man you were. And I, uh, appreciate how you've helped her at the museum."

"Happy to do it." Blake studied his father a moment. He was being surprisingly open and forthright. Maybe now was a good time to share what he knew about Mark's behavior. "Dad, there are things I discovered."

Owen held up a hand to forestall him. "I know what Mark did. I knew he bought that company and I know I pushed him to do it. I'd convinced myself he was brilliant enough to make the whole thing work. He was always so smart with the business." His shoulders sagged. "But it didn't take long to see it was a big mistake, but I chose to ignore it. I had every confidence in my son. Eventually I realized the problem was too big to fix, but I couldn't accept that Mark wasn't perfect. Or that he might be to blame for the whole mess. The realization was too much. Jackie thinks it might have been the cause of my heart attack."

"So all this time you knew and didn't say anything. Didn't warn Norman."

Owen looked at him, his eyes glimmering with pain

and regret. "I couldn't face the fact that my perfect son was destroying my family's business."

"What brought this change about, Dad?"

"When Jackie quit, I started to see what I'd been doing. Then when I saw the damage at the museum and knew you were there, I realized I could lose you, too. I didn't want that. I'd been focusing on a false legacy and ignored the real one right in front of me. You and Eden and Lucy." He stared at his hands a moment. "Pride is a terrible sin. It got in the way of all my relationships. I'm going to try and guard against that going forward. I have a second chance with Jackie, and I'd like a second chance with you, too, son."

"I never meant to hurt you, Dad, I just—"

Owen stood. "Had to live your own life. I see that now. I've been blind and selfish. I hope we can start over. I…I've missed you, son."

Blake's throat tightened. "I'd like that. I've missed you, too."

Owen stepped forward, opened his arms and hugged him. Tears welled up in Blake's eyes. Never in his wildest dreams had he ever imagined this kind of reconciliation with his father. The Lord truly did move in mysterious ways.

"Well, I'd better get back to the house. Jackie will be wondering where I am."

Blake shut the door and walked back into the bedroom. His half-filled duffel mocked him. Eden was right. He'd been walking away because it was easier than trying to talk things through with her.

If he wanted another chance with Eden, then he'd have to set aside his normal way of addressing a situation and allow her to participate in their decision about their future.

Blake wrestled with his predicament through the night and into the morning. However, after a lot of tossing and turning, he'd finally realized that the only way to talk to Eden was to let her lead the way. He waited until she returned from dropping Lucy off at school before he went to the main house.

She turned away when he entered the kitchen. "I thought you'd be gone by now."

"No. I have a few important things to take care of first."

She shrugged. "Well, I wouldn't know because you never tell anyone what you're going to do."

"Not this time. I need your help."

"You're a Sinclair." She huffed out a breath. "They don't ask for help, remember?"

"I'm a Sinclair but I'm asking for your help. Please, Eden."

She faced him, a puzzled look in her eyes. "Why?"

"Because I'm stuck, and I don't know how to move forward. You're the only one who can help me."

"I doubt that." She crossed her arms over her chest. "So, what do you want?"

"Will you take a walk with me?"

She glanced outside. "It's nice out. I suppose…"

They started at the end of the drive near the garage and took the path toward the rear of the property. "Where are we going?"

"To my favorite spot."

"I didn't know you had one."

"I'd forgotten about it until last night." They walked across the lawn, stopping near a copse of trees beside the stream that ran along the edge of the property. "When I was a kid, we owned another five acres back there. My view wasn't marred by homes then."

He turned and moved to a large tree whose main trunk had split into four and provided a cozy hollow in the center. "I used to come here and sit when I needed to think things through."

Eden smiled. "I don't think you'll fit anymore."

"No. But there's a fallen log near the stream." He took her hand and steered her through the trees. He helped her up on the log and then sat beside her. "My dad came to see me yesterday. We've made our peace. I thought you'd like to know."

She clutched his arm. "That's wonderful, Blake. I'm happy for you."

"Which means I have a decision to make. One I can't, no, *won't* make without getting your input."

"Since when?"

"Since it involves you. And me. And Lucy." He took her hand. "I want us to be a family. A real family. I love you and I love that little girl."

Eden looked away. "Blake, what about...?"

"Don't. It's time to remove the obstacles. I know we've both been held back by guilt, troubled by the fact that I'm Mark's brother. I learned a long time ago that friends come and go in our lives for a reason. When that reason is fulfilled, we drift apart and move on to a new friendship. Why not the same for spouses? Your marriage to my brother was exactly what you both needed, and you made a life and a child together. But he's gone now and you're free to move on and love again. I admit I've been feeling like I'm stealing something from Mark. That I somehow was dishonoring his life if I loved you."

"And now?"

"I'm asking you to marry me and let me give you and Lucy the life you deserve."

"Where would we start this new life?"

"I don't know yet. At the moment I have no job and no prospects." He leaned toward her and framed her face with his hands. "All I know is that I don't want to spend another day without the two of you in my life. We'll trust the Lord to work out the details. He's pretty good at that sort of thing."

"Yes, I know. I asked Him to remove you from my life at one point. Thankfully, He just laughed at my request."

"Is that a yes?"

She answered him with a kiss, one with no reservations or restraints, a kiss just for him.

A short while later they started back toward the house. Blake held her hand, unwilling to let go. Ever.

Eden slowed her steps as they neared the backyard. "I need to tell Lucy. She'll be so happy."

Blake stopped. "What about Mark? He'll always be her father."

She touched his chest. "Yes, and we can both keep his memory alive for her by sharing our memories of him."

"We'll have to tell Jackie and Owen eventually. I don't want to ruin his happy mood with this. He might be violently against us. Mark will always be his favorite son."

Eden squeezed his hand. "No. He was simply the oldest son."

"There you are."

Blake and Eden looked up to see Owen walking toward them. Blake braced himself. "Uh-oh."

He stopped and studied them a moment, then nodded and looked at Blake. "I have something for you. I'm glad I found you together." He reached into his pocket and pulled out a piece of paper.

Blake frowned at the number written on there. "What is it?"

"It's the phone number for the human resources office at the academy in Mobile. Call them first thing tomorrow and they'll tell you when to report to work."

Stunned, Blake struggled to grasp what his dad had done. "How did you know?"

Owen winked at Eden. "Someone who cares for you told me about the sacrifices you've made and were willing to make recently."

"I don't understand. I turned the job down."

His father shrugged. "I know some people, made a few calls. They hadn't filled the position yet, so I reminded them of your special qualifications. It didn't take much persuading, so I assume you're a more accomplished man than I ever imagined."

"You know this means we'll be moving to Mobile."

Owen nodded. "I know how to get there. Jackie loves Orange Beach."

Blake tugged Eden closer to his side. "Dad, there's something else..."

Owen held up his hand. "I know. I've known for a while now. You can't keep a thing like that hidden for long."

Blake glanced at Eden. "And you're okay with us?"

"I got a second chance at love. You two deserve the same."

Eden broke free of his hand and wrapped Owen in a hug. "Thank you. You've made us very happy."

Jackie and Lucy came toward them across the lawn. Lucy darted forward and ran to hug Blake. Jackie stopped at Owen's side, a huge smile on her face. "Aha. I see you two finally have come to terms with things. About time. I never saw two people so much in love."

Owen scowled. "Hey."

"Besides us that is. Come on, Owen. Let these love-birds have some privacy to celebrate."

Eden stooped down to speak to her daughter. "Lucy, how would you like to have Uncle Blake live with us all the time? He'd be your new daddy."

She smiled and nodded, lifting an adoring glance at Blake. She thought a moment, her forehead creased. "Will I have two daddies now? The one in heaven and him?"

Eden smiled. "Yes."

"I have to tell Cuddles." She ran off, and Eden stood, slipping her arm around Blake's waist.

"It looks like the family is in agreement."

"Are you okay with moving to Mobile?"

She nodded. "They have old houses there I can help save."

"And maybe live in. We'll find a big old house that needs love, and you can fill it with all the antique furniture and chandeliers you want." He grinned. "And maybe a few kids."

"Oh? How many?"

Blake shrugged. "Six or seven."

"Whoa, cowboy. How about we start small, like a brother and sister for Lucy."

"Deal." He pulled her into his arms. "Wherever we end up, I'll be happy and content as long as we're all together."

Eden touched his cheek and placed a kiss on his lips. "I'm so glad you came home, my prodigal lawman."

Blake held her close to his heart and sent up a prayer of gratitude. Yesterday his life was a pile of rubble at his feet. Today he had a future and a family.

God truly did work in mysterious ways.

* * * * *

Dear Reader,

Pride, forgiveness and guilt are all things humans struggle with. Blake Sinclair faces all three when he returns home after a long absence. An unforgiving father and the lovely widow of his older brother complicate things even more. It takes patience and much understanding to work through all the obstacles Blake and Eden face. One by one they are able to break down the barriers.

We all grow impatient and frustrated when things don't go as we plan. Sometimes the best solution is to just take a step back, inhale a deep breath and wait to see what the next day brings. We have to resist our need to take matters into our own hands and allow the Lord to unfold events as He has them laid out.

For Blake and Eden it provides a happy ending and a path around the guilt. For others in the story it provides peace and a new beginning from pride that can destroy a family. Waiting on the Lord is the only way to overcome the difficult parts of life because love is always the answer.

I love to hear from my readers. You can follow me on FB at Lorraine Beatty Author or on Twitter @lorraine_beatty.

Lorraine

COMING NEXT MONTH FROM
Love Inspired

THE AMISH MARRIAGE ARRANGEMENT
Amish Country Matches • by Patricia Johns
Sarai Peachy is convinced that her *grossmammi* and their next-door neighbor are the perfect match. But the older man's grandson isn't so sure. When a storm forces the two to work together on repairs, will spending time with Arden Stoltzfus prove to Sarai that the former heartbreaker is a changed man?

THE AMISH NANNY'S PROMISE
by Amy Grochowski
Since the loss of his wife, Nick Weaver has relied on nanny Fern Beiler to care for him and his *kinner*. But when the community pushes them into a marriage of convenience, the simple arrangement grows more complicated. Will these two friends find love for a lifetime?

HER ALASKAN COMPANION
K-9 Companions • by Heidi McCahan
Moving to Alaska is the fresh start that pregnant widow Lexi Thomas has been looking for. But taking care of a rambunctious dog wasn't part of the plan. When an unlikely friendship blooms between her and the dog's owner, Heath Donovan, can she take a chance and risk her heart again?

THE RELUCTANT RANCHER
Lone Star Heritage • by Jolene Navarro
World-weary FBI agent Enzo Flores returns home to help his pregnant sister. When she goes into premature labor, he needs help to care for his nephew and the ranch. Will childhood rival Resa Espinoza step in to help and forgive their troubled past?

FALLING FOR THE FAMILY NEXT DOOR
Sage Creek • by Jennifer Slattery
Needing a fresh start, Daria Ellis moves to Texas with her niece and nephew. But it's more challenging than she ever imagined, especially with handsome cowboy Tyler Reyes living next door. When they clash over property lines, will it ruin everything or prove to be a blessing in disguise?

A HAVEN FOR HIS TWINS
by April Arrington
Deciding to right the wrongs of the past, former bull rider Holt Williams returns home to reclaim his twin sons. But Jessie Alden, the woman who's raised them all these years, isn't keen on the idea. Can he be trusted, or will he hurt his sons—and her—all over again?

LICNM0623

HARLEQUIN
PLUS

Try the best multimedia subscription service for romance readers like you!

Read, Watch and Play.

Experience the easiest way to get the romance content you crave.

Start your **FREE TRIAL** at
<u>www.harlequinplus.com/freetrial</u>.